I0668988

QUANTUM CHRONICLES II

ANTHONY FUCILLA

Published 2024 by arima publishing

www.arimapublishing.com

ISBN 978 1 84549 836 8
© Anthony Fucilla 2024

Swirl is an imprint of arima publishing.

arima publishing
ASK House, Northgate Avenue
Bury St Edmunds, Suffolk IP32 6BB
t: (+44) 01284 717884

www.arimapublishing.com

13 Short Stories

Quantum Chronicles
In The Eleventh
Dimension 2

ANTHONY FUCILLA

Cover Design: Gary Pope
Editor: Vicky Cheyne Sheppard

CONTENTS

Introduction

Quantum Chronicles 2 is a book comprised of 13 short stories. The very first story I wrote was 'Destination Citon', a story which appears later in the book. The main theme is, 'What is reality? Does the mind construct reality? How much of what we call reality is actually real?'

After a time of much reflection, I was inexorably compelled to choose my first story for the book, 'At Your Request'. This is a story that leaves us with a profound philosophical question, an essential question, one that we may have failed to tackle, but one that demands an answer if we are to be certain of ourselves and our place in this amazing world... 'What is it to be human? Is it the planet we are born on? Is it our appearance, our mind, that has the neurological capacity to create wonders, or is there something far deeper and more significant that lies within each one of us; perhaps something a finely tuned robot is devoid of, along with the animal kingdom, which coexists around us?' This is the question I leave you with, in the hope that you find an answer. Perhaps in it lies the key to life... the very key to our existence.

> "All the stories are excellent and provide much food for thought but the two (The Appointment/ Memoirs of Time) are, for me at least, outstanding in both content and the implications they contain for us all now in this very real materialistic world of ours..."

Professor Jeremy Dunning-Davies
Physicist and Mathematician

Man is held within the sphere of Time and Space but beyond it lies another realm

At Your Request
William Leadholm, widower, on the verge of suicide, heads to Earth, where he can have his late wife reconstructed to his exact specifications

The Memory of Green
Sean Winters, lunar resident, pursues a lifetime dream when he travels to Earth. With limited time he sets out to unfold its mysteries

The Man Who Awoke Yesterday
Dirk Allen awakens in unfamiliar surroundings and soon faces a brutal reality as his very own existence is now called into question

Slit in the Sky
Crazed Scientist, Eric Western, manufacturer of the T-Propeller, is on a quest to prove that all life on earth originated from aliens

The Appointment
The planet Orious sits uniquely in deep space. Ludovic Martel, Terra Ambassador, meets with its leader with an unexpected message

The Hidden Cave
Deep beneath the sea lies a doorway into a parallel dimension. Cliff Fontaine soon discovers this when his world is turned upside down. Is there a way back?

Terra Unknown
Commander Kubo Van den Berg arrives on an unknown planet, one far out in another solar system where nothing but the relics of a past existence remains

Destination Citon
Lotto winner Ed Rutherford suddenly awakens

Spy Hunter
Beyond the confines of a subterranean world, mutants stalk the surface of the radioactive earth with an unwanted guest

Mind Blitz
In a world where your thoughts and ideas are no longer your own, people who set out to conceal them are deemed evil

Memoirs of Time
Boris Muller finds the key to unlock the gateway of time

He Dreams Planet Earth
Mind Control: the ultimate crime prevention

The Edge of Eternity
At death what happens to that invisible energy of the brain known as consciousness?

At Your Request

Speeding down a steel state highway, William Leadholm sat in a surface-cab, contemplating the babble of his own thoughts as they echoed through his mind. Ahead stretched a vast panorama; a sun-shimmering metropolis now slowly coming into view as the robot driver increased velocity.

"How far to go...?" William exclaimed in an unsteady nervous tone, cigarette clamped between his teeth.

The robot referred to the time distance indicator on the gleaming control board:

"Five scheduled minutes..."

The surface-cab arrived, halting smoothly, and pressing his hand against the credit register, William stepped out, dashing towards a grey-domed building. Reading the luminous indication map he made his way up the stairs, two at a time. It helped that he vaguely recalled the way, even though a year had passed. He caught sight of the flashing arrowed sign, '*Love Reunited.*' Throwing his weight against the heavy white door, he entered the main reception. Robot workers and humans filled the lobby going about their daily activities. In the last two years, Earth had become a planet infested with machines; statistically there were more robots than humans but in this moment, with his sole objective in mind, he gazed around, almost dismissing the scene.

A robot nurse came over towards him holding a tray of metallic components. A name lay across the bundle,

'*Mrs S. Jones.*' He loosened his collar, licking his lips. He tried to dismiss the thought that Cindy would have been nothing more than that pile of metal it was holding; similar components. His attention returned to the robot now standing face to face with him shaking her head, her photocell eyes narrowing down his image.

"No smoking Sir... See the sign?"

"I'm sorry, just a little anxious."

He felt two spots of red glowing on his cheeks. Swallowing hard, he dropped his cigarette to the floor, stamping on it with his heel.

"Are you here to see someone?"

"Yes, yes, I am. Doctor Nash. I'm five minutes late already."

His anxiety was building, manifesting in his posture, voice, and trembling hands.

"Down the hall to your right... at the far end, you can't miss it."

Pushing on with tunnel-like vision, he pierced through the endless tide of activity. Nothing could deflect him from this long- awaited moment which had now arrived. Reaching the door, it opened mechanically.

"Mr Leadholm, please enter," a calm sophisticated voice requested.

He stepped in, battling with his emotions. His heartbeat began to increase. Doctor Nash was sitting in a chair; he was a highly advanced robot constructed in humanoid form, clothed in an immaculate dark blue suit. He had the physical appearance of a man right down to the last detail, with an intellectual insight and faculty way beyond that of a human being, unlike the other finely assembled metallic workers. He was slim with refined features, his eyes dark green, his cheeks freckled, but something about his voice was peculiar, the one flaw in such a perfect construction.

"It's been quite a while, a year to the day in fact. How was your trip from Krutopa? Still busy building space stations there I take it?"

"Yes, indeed…"

"You're the Technical Director aren't you?"

"Doc, please, I can't wait anymore…"

"Patience, relax! She's ready for you."

"Where is it then?"

"It…!"

"Well, it is a robot, is it not? Just like you, just like all of you." He clenched his fists, dots of sweat surfacing across his forehead.

"Come now, Mr Leadholm, what's gotten into you?"

The Doctor stood up, walked over to him, guiding him into a chair in front of the desk. William hung his head, glaring sullenly at the floor.

"It appears to me you are still very confused, neurotic, very emotionally unbalanced. I hope you are ready for this."

The Doctor sat crossing his legs, regarding him with sharp eyed perspicacity.

"Are you?"

There was a moment of penetrating silence.

"As you know, at this agency we place emphasis on psychological release with all our clients. It appears you're still suffering from periodic bouts of depression. You've had a whole year of therapy back on Krutopa."

He paused...

"Remember it's all a question of psychology, cognitive psychology, conditioning of the mind. Clearly your view of robots is still distorted and negative, but regardless of that, if you believe she's real, real she is. Objectively maybe not, but who cares what most humans think...? It's the subjective approach that counts. If she is real to you nothing else should matter."

The doctor sat back tilting his chair convinced of his own existence... convinced he too was alive and real.

"Mr Leadholm, I suggest that you don't philosophise too much, it will do you no good. Trust me, in a month or so you won't even recall this discussion... besides, legally, she's alive."

The words reverberated around the room.

"Does it know... sorry, she?" William asked flatly.

"Know what?"

"That she's a robot...?"

"How could she not know what she is? Aesthetically she's as human as can be, identical to your late wife Cindy both in appearance and character... even her voice has been modified to that of your wife. The air compressed voice disc is very special."

'*Too bad yours isn't,*' William thought cynically.

"Tell me Doc, will she really have the same characteristics... I mean in every way?"

"Yes Sir, just as you requested... kind and sweet with all the other qualities Cindy had, minus the negatives of course."

William grinned, the words thundering in his ears.

"She will not nag and whine or give conflicting orders. She will be submissive at all times, an altruist, a giver in all ways."

"What about her memory... all the ones I shared with Cindy?"

"She will have none. Although she knows who you are, her husband, she will be devoid of all the memories you and Cindy shared. It's a completely new start. She will need to learn about you, her home, etc. Teach her the ways, share your experiences. A fresh new chapter awaits you both."

"Will she die?"

"Everything ceases to be Mr Leadholm, biological and mechanical. It's the cycle of life, the universal law. Nothing can stand against the force of time."

"But... but she must have a basic life expectancy."

"Of course, sixty years of longevity, beyond that point she will cease to be. Considering you're thirty-six, she should outlive you. The other plus is that she will never have to experience that awful decaying process that all you humans go through as you age. But anyway this is all academic. Above all she will love you, unconditionally."

"Really?" William muttered. His eyes lit with anticipation.

"Yes, really Sir. I've spoken with and examined her meticulously. She's a wonderful woman, highly intelligent, very engaging but you need to give her time to adjust to the world, especially on Krutopa, so please be patient."

"You know Doc, it isn't easy when you've lost someone you love. Death is hard to take, especially after six years of marriage. I was close to ending my life had it not been for..."

"Us? Love Reunited?" You can put all those painful memories aside. You came to us a year ago, the only legalised planet in the entire galaxy to indulge in such a practice... travelled fifty-eight thousand light years to Earth, as you have now, in order to get back the woman you love. Well, she's ready for you."

William let his breath out in weightless relief.

"Just as well there are no laws prohibiting her living on Krutopa."

The doctor smiled, tapping his fingers on the glazed desktop.

"Before we go any further, there are a few routine documents that you have to fill out and sign."

From a drawer, he produced the relevant papers, with them a pen.

"If you would please..."

Hurriedly, William read through them, almost dismissively, nervously filling out each section. He just wanted to see her... it... her!

"Okay Doc, all done."

He shifted the pile over, dropping the pen on top. He had regained strength and mental equilibrium, evident by the gleam in his eyes. The Doctor flipped rapidly through the sheets, analysing. His photocell brain operating at high velocity, relays and memory banks clicking. Switches activated internally, allowing a surge of electricity to flow.

"Okay Mr Leadholm, you've waited long enough."

The wall behind the doctor faded, turning from a white solid concrete block to transparent. They were now looking into a brightly lit room. There was motion and sound, faint but definite. William watched on critically, his heartbeat increasing. He felt slightly faint. With a hum the walls parted from the centre point, like an opening curtain. There, standing before them was Cindy, dressed in a white medical robe, a robot technician by her side. The Doctor motioned them forward. William rose, mouth gaping. She was perfect, identical to the very inch. Her face was well chiselled and pale, velvety-like skin, her eyes cold blue, hair dark brown, almost black, her feet petite and sculptured.

"Cindy... Cindy."

He raced over and held her, squeezing her with emotion, years of pain and heartache fading. She was warm and substantial, her white robe rustling as she moved against him.

"William, Oh William..." She looked into his eyes dreamily, breathless and excited. "We have so much to see, so much to do."

Her supple arms circled his neck, her red lips delicate and moist.

"Yes sweetheart. Now that we are together, I'm complete. You have given me a reason to live. Come, we have two days left here. Friday we leave for Krutopa."

"Krutopa? How faraway is it?" she asked, letting the word roll and spin around her mechanical brain.

"Fifty-eight thousand light years away, in another region of this galaxy, miraculously discovered seventy years back. A clean, beautiful virgin land, with an ocean, eroded cliffs and mountains, forests, rivers and waterfalls, landscapes... the magnificence of which you couldn't imagine. There are many colonists there, families from all over the galaxy."

Her eyes sparkled with excitement, an inner innocence. The doctor pulled the blinds eradicating the sunlight which had now filtered through. The room sank into an amber glow. William pulled away from her gently, stepping towards the doctor.

"Thank you" he said, peering over his shoulder at his lovely Cindy. "I don't know what to say."

He blushed, his face contorted with emotion, pulled out of its natural form by inner forces and feelings.

"Mr Leadholm, remember this all happened because of you. It was done at your request."

The doctor signalled to the robot technician. He turned, holding Cindy by the hand, walking her back inside the room, silent and efficient. With a thump the wall transformed back into a solid white concrete block.

"Hey, where's she going...?"

"Patience Sir. She needs to get dressed. She'll be with you in around five minutes."

The doctor smiled warmly, rubbing his hands with satisfaction. Task accomplished. It was complete. There was a knock, a metallic head popped around the door as it opened.

"Doctor Nash, I've got a Mr Watson in reception, a human. He's pretty bad."

"Okay nurse, see him through."

"Well, that's that, I guess," William said excitedly.

"Remember Mr Leadholm, in a year's time you are scheduled to return here, a relationship check-up review if you like. A one off but it's paramount. Now if you wouldn't mind waiting in reception, I have another client."

He tapped his wrist at his vid-watch. Perceiving the hint William turned for the door.

"Thanks Doc. Thanks for everything."

Stepping out into a world of commotion and activity, William took in a breath of fresh air, Cindy close by, warm sunlight streaming down on them. Gazing ahead, they digested the scene. The huge rumbling city of Los Angeles was crammed with people moving along the streets, chatting, walking into shops, bars, parks, and buildings. Surface vehicles filled the roads buzzing by; interplanetary jets moved above in the atmosphere, flashing projectiles of metal in suspension and blistering motion. A section of the city rose high, skyscrapers piercing the clouds. Cindy's eyes roamed like a lost child, getting to grips with the complex tangle and confusion of the world.

"Wow, the city is beautiful, isn't it?"

"Yes sweetheart, it is indeed."

They walked on leisurely, strolling hand in hand like two juveniles gripped in teenage love. Then, from the corner of his eye, William spotted a cab. Waving it down, it drew up instantly beside the curb.

"Where to?" the robot driver inquired.

"Aphrodite Hotel."

They jumped in and the surface-cab zipped off turning a corner, spiralling cautiously towards the underground highway.

In the dim amber light of the hotel bar, William and Cindy sat, eyes fixed on each other intently, a shared hungry look. The bar was located under the sea, the only section of the hotel sub-aqua. The ambience was warm, soft, alternating lights flickering across the floor and beautifully sculptured ceiling. It resembled an ancient Greek temple. In the background music played, instrumental with a mystical Arabian beat.

"Waiter," William signalled, catching a view of the dense pacific waters which engulfed them in the circular structured bar. For a brief moment he saw a large fish through the glass. A robot waitress approached.

"Yes Sir, what can I get you?" She held the com-board patiently waiting for the order.

"Two chocolate flavoured coffees."

He looked over at Cindy, smiling.

"Extra cream in one please," he murmured dreamily.

William leaned towards her, his elbow resting against the table which diffused a pale green light. It spread over his features.

"You always loved it that way."

He smiled to himself, lost temporarily in nostalgic thought. Memories... There was no response from her, other than a bashful smile.

"Tell me William, tell me about yourself."

"What do you want to know?"

"Anything... everything..."

She reached over, holding his hand, her nails well-manicured and exquisitely tapered, eyes glowing with interest.

"Back home I'm the Technical Director of an engineering company. We build space stations."

"What about the planet itself, Krutopa? Is life there like it is here?"

"Every planet has to keep pace..."

"With?"

"With the general trend of galactic culture, which was formulated here on Earth, the central source, but yes of course there are some inevitable differences, legal ones for sure."

Abruptly, the robot waitress placed the tray of coffees on the table, severing the flow of the conversation. *'Damn robots!'* he thought, *'no matter how sophisticated they are they simply lack that human touch.'* Ironically, overwhelmed by passion, he had almost forgotten that Cindy was inorganic.

"If you would, please Sir..."

He pressed his finger against the credit register. The tiny device clicked and flashed.

"Thank you. Enjoy."

"I'm sorry, where was I?" he said, moving the tray into the centre of the table.

"Have you travelled much? I mean in this solar system."

She lifted the mug of choc-coffee, taking a few cautious sips.

"Yes, as a matter of fact, I have."

For a moment he paused overwhelmed by flickering waves of emotion.

"I've been to Mars several times. Interestingly the distance between Earth and Mars is variable, due to their elliptical orbits around the sun. The gravity is much weaker on Mars, never liked it though... nothing going on, just mountains, a few bars and restaurants, lots of construction, and the locals were very grumpy."

"Anywhere else?" She licked her lips, the froth melting away into liquid.

"The moon, Lunar. It's close by, Earth's only natural satellite."

"Wow."

"Unfortunately most of the planets in this system are uninhabitable that's why I've always hated it here. Venus is volcanic... just lava and steam, way too hot. As for the gigantic planets like Jupiter and Saturn, they are nothing but giant balls of gas without a conventional solid surface. Besides, you would be crushed on entry and to date no known metal can withstand such pressure."

In the brief silence that followed, William was caught, hypnotised by her beauty. It was surreal; everything about her was identical to his wife, the posture, the look, the slight motion of her body.

"What's Lunar like?" she asked, breaking his stunned gaze.

"Lunar?"

He raised his hands expressively, masking his feelings.

"An indoor existence... huge oxygen pumped cities. In general the people there are a lot taller and thinner as a result of the moon's weak gravitational field. Environment and gravity play a key role in how humans evolve physically, genetically."

Her face lit with enthusiasm as the information filtered through.

"I see that my experiences fascinate you." His voice was faint but passionate. She blushed. Her eyes sparkled, alive with emotion.

"How long were you there?"

"Two months. I worked there during college break, needed the extra cash, good rates. I guess that's why I eventually left Earth."

She leaned back crossing her legs. A cloud of cigarette smoke drifted by, sucked automatically towards the fume detector across the ceiling.

"Here you spend most of your life working for just a few credits. The virgin planets in contrast pay well, handsomely, that's why very few humans now remain here. Most live on Andradome."

"Andradome?"

"It's in my solar system, furthest one out. I've been there. It's pretty rough. Annual periodic meteor swarms, constant bad weather but plenty of unlimited opportunities. It's even being nicknamed the golden globe."

"Was it always like that?"

"No, it took time for it to develop, time before a rational working system was implemented. Originally the locals were very withdrawn, almost tribal, a decentralized society locked into their own way of thinking... the best way!"

His eyes rolled sardonically.

"I guess it's because they are so far out, cut off a little. It was a society that initially rejected the advanced technocratic and cultural commodities of the galaxy. Even now some still want independence. Took years before the government signed the U.G.C Articles."

He cut off sharply.

"I'm probably boring you, right? I'm sorry. I guess I'm so taken aback by everything. Usually when I'm nervous I rattle on, get lost in my own world... was like that as a kid."

"You're not boring me. Nothing you say or do, could ever."

"But surely you must have certain likes and dislikes. Don't you?"

"Your desires are my desires... your dreams are my dreams."

The reality of her nature once again penetrated his daze. William fought it, regaining composure. She reached over and held his hand mesmerised, gazing at him profoundly. They both smiled a smile of complete understanding.

"Tell me, will it take long to reach Krutopa?"

"No it's very quick. Once we've ascended into a certain point in space we enter a wormhole. It's basically a shortcut through space and time. Wormholes allow you to travel from one point of the universe to another in an instant. That's how we reach planets light years away. Our galaxy, the Milky Way is enormous you know, approximately one hundred thousand light years in diameter."

"What did you study in college? You appear to have quite an intellect."

"Come on, it's basic stuff."

She chuckled in amusement.

"I studied engineering, but I always loved philosophy, metaphysics. I dabbled a bit here and there. Theories of ultimate reality, purpose of life."

"You know, William we are going to be so happy together."

Her eyelashes flickered modestly, her chiselled face well marked out in the dim light.

"I love you more than anything, more than life. This is meant to be."

Overcome for a moment, all he could see were her lips moving, no sound coming at all, eradicated by languid dream-like thoughts which rippled through his mind.

"Yes Cindy. I've always loved you. Things are going to be just perfect. This is only the beginning."

A year elapsed.

"Doctor Nash, Mr Leadholm is here for his relationship check-up review. He's sitting in your office. His file is on your desk."

"Thank you, nurse," he said smiling at her.

Doctor Nash walked into his office and studied his client intuitively. Relays and memory banks clicked.

"Mr Leadholm, good to see you again. It's been a year to the day. Here for your relationship check-up review. The year has flown by."

He sat down facing William and quickly flicked through the file on his desk.

"So how have things progressed with you?" The doctor consulted his vid-watch, pushing back his shirt sleeve. "How are things with Mrs Leadholm?"

William dabbed his forehead with a hanky and shifted around on his chair a few times in a series of nervous motions. He appeared withdrawn, drained of life and energy.

"Not so good Doctor Nash."

The doctor frowned, almost shocked.

"Really? Why? She loves you. Does she not?"

"Oh yes, there's no doubt about that."

"Well, what's the problem then?" He raised both hands.

"Just that."

"Just what Mr Leadholm?" The pitch in his voice rose.

"Doctor, it isn't real."

"It...! We've discussed this already. Remember it's a question of psychology."

"It hasn't even adjusted to the human scent."

"Mr Leadholm, it took me sometime to do so."

William's eyes grew wide with cold twisting fury.

"You're ignoring reality Doctor. Humans and machines are totally different. A maze of wires cannot replace a beating heart. I've acquired a pet, nothing more than a pet. Even then, most pets are disobedient. She just follows and agrees with everything I say and do. She has no personality of her own, none whatsoever. There is a distinct bias in everything she says and does in order to fit into my way of thinking."

"And? You wanted unconditional love, did you not?"

"This isn't that. Cindy doesn't love. It has no sense of the actual meaning. Real love, natural love is something else. It's programmed, an artificial life source, imitating a far superior life form. It's a machine, made up of mathematical algorithms, bits of programming logic that govern the very mechanisms of its robotic brain. Its sentiments are nothing but programs, electrical signals whizzing through it so that it corresponds to certain actions and emotions. Doctor Nash it's a machine, a highly advanced machine."

"Sir," The doctor banged his fist against the glazed desk sending a few sheets of paper drifting to the ground.

"As a humanoid I take offence. That distortion you have lodged in your mind hasn't seemed to have left you. You came here with one objective."

Slowly he began to regain composure.

"We fulfilled our task. We gave her to you real or not and worked frantically around your specifications. If it is true love you're in search of, human love as you call it, well I'm afraid that is out of my jurisdiction."

"True love," William muttered under his breath. "Human love, it's biological, it stems from the soul, it lies deep within us, within the very fabric of man. It's an abstract emotion displayed by actions, deeds. It can't be bought or manufactured; it's something that no machine can mimic. It's a very special gift."

"Indeed, Mr Leadholm, indeed. But what is it to be human? What is it to be alive? Whether programmed or not she acts, responds, does, says, loves. Who cares how those feelings and emotions are induced or generated. Who's to say that you as a human are not somehow programmed yourself?"

He cut off emphatically.

"I think that'll be all," William said, getting to his feet. "Nothing can bring her back. Perhaps in time the scars will heal, perhaps not."

"Time Mr Leadholm, time will indeed be your only friend, in these circumstances at least, but then again, there are some things in time that will never erode or indeed be forgotten."

The Memory of Green

Accelerating to its maximum velocity, L-11 ascended towards the darkness of space, its lights flashing like fire, sweeping across the lunar surface. Gaining altitude promptly, the face of the globe grew smaller, the space-station disappearing, fading into a meaningless speck. Through vocal activation, Sean flicked through the various channels in search of entertainment. *Mundane and boring*, he thought until channel 7 captured his attention. Before his eyes, narrated by the ubiquitous Professor Kepplar, was a virtual space tour. An unknown planet suddenly revolved around the screen, one which was located in a different region of galaxy. The image then magnified, displaying its lifeless, sun baked steaming volcanic landscape. Fiddling with the aud-dial, he looked on with growing interest. 'Fascinating,' he muttered under his breath until the image began to slowly fade. Wave interference... blank.

"Miss...oh miss," he rasped, waving his arm to acquire the attention of the blond stewardess, who instantly acknowledged his signal. Having caught her attention, he lowered his arm, eyes full of expectancy.

"How can I help Sir?"

Against the grey of her jacket, he noticed her name in bold white letters.

"Sandrine, there's no transmission." He indicated the blank screen with a sweep of his hand.

"Sorry Sir, it does occur regularly. As we leave the moon's gravitational field there are sometimes minor problems with the entertainment broadcasting signal, give it a few minutes."

Smiling brightly she turned, making her way down the aisle of the ship, appeasing the other passengers with her sensitive attention. Dismissing the matter, Sean glanced through the side-window, his destination on his mind. Far out in the distance, he caught sight of it; the blue rotating sphere, Earth, as he had done from his lunar-base countless times before. It hung there, frozen in time like a striking precious jewel, enclosed in its own blue bubble of atmosphere and activity, manufacturing and breathing its own oxygen. '*Blue,*' he thought, '*a vast ocean, an endless expanse of water... life.*' This excited him. He recalled the images he had seen via powerful telescope, the sun shimmering, dancing across the cold waters of the Pacific and Atlantic. With a nervous hand, he adjusted the flow of oxygen, twisting a dial above his head, gripped by both fear and wonder; two conflicting emotions.

Time stretched... L-11 assumed an orbit outside the gravity belt of the planet, a blazing mass of white lighting the trackless void.

In the Customs lounge of the New York State space-station, Sean walked through, bag in hand, his green attire blending in with the other lunar passengers. The station itself was filled with luminous pillars, positioned mathematically in all directions in order to maintain and support the alloys which evidently made up the structure. Gazing around like a lost child in search of direction, he felt lonely and fearful, yet his surging curiosity was enough to quench and nullify those impeding emotions which threatened to overwhelm him. After years of pent-up desire, he had finally come to the place, the place where earthly reality had been nothing more than a dream, until now.

Approaching the Check-Port, Sean held out his hand. A small metallic machine stood there functioning homeostatically, orienting itself under human supervision. It would roll slightly forward then backwards on its four metal wheels, registering passenger by passenger, supplying itself with the necessary data. On the odd occasion it would bleep, indicating no admission. The cycle repeated itself in rhythmic motion. It was now Sean's turn.

"Next," a security guard mumbled.

With his hand raised, he aligned himself with the machine, marked out by a yellow line across the floor. The cycle at once commenced. From a tiny aperture, it emitted a wink of red light as it began to roll forward. Its trajectory was spot on as it met with his coded hand, depositing his information as a permanent record within its rapidly operating complex system.

Now, slightly aggravated, he passed under an arc screen, phase two of the monitoring process a DNA data collector. In a fraction of a second it removed a hair follicle from his scalp, storing it accordingly.

The exit now came into view as he looked ahead through towering glass doors. He could see people, earth people, massed together in chaos and confusion, clothed in a variety of colours, something which the lunar residents were not accustomed to. How he wished he had someone waiting for him. It was just him alone, alone to face the untamed world of earthly existence. His relatives spoke continually of its beauty, but also of its danger and ugliness. He recalled the words of his grandfather, *'Sean, Earth is a jungle like no other, the animals who dwell there, live and act on predatory instinct, but Man, earthly Man is a cocktail of unpredictabilities, good and evil, highs and lows, their behavioural patterns constantly altering in untimely sporadic bursts. Unlike an animal, the duality of man is unique.'* He smiled, recapturing the moment fully; he could almost picture his grandfather as if it were the other day, mumbling these words at the lunar base. With the clenching of a fist, as if to transmit courage to himself, he muttered, "I will blend in... I will get to grips with this world, surely."

Stepping out of the space-station, into the open atmosphere, he took in his first deep breath of air. It felt good, his nostrils flaring as he inhaled again. Instantly he detected the scent of flowers commingling with the foul odours of the city. He smiled, looking into the blue, gazing towards the sun, its heat and radiance penetrating into his depths warming him inwardly, an experience that he had been devoid of. *'Lunar was radically different,'* he thought, making sharp, brief comparisons in his jaded mind. Up above, life was an enclosed existence, fuelled by canned oxygen which was perpetually pumped into the lunar structures. Beyond the confines of the indoor world, it was lifeless, bleak and hostile, a globe without atmosphere due to its small mass and consequently insufficient gravitational field. A landscape filled with gaping craters formed by explosive impacts of high velocity asteroids... comets. Adjusting to the Earth's gravity was

24

only going to be a minor problem; after all, the lunar cities simulated Earth-like gravity had conditioned him for the real thing.

Gripped by awe, he walked onto a patch of muddy soil gazing at a tiny spider. He pointed and laughed, amazed by what he saw, recalling his brief lessons in entomology. Kneeling, he placed his hand by it, surveying its motion; it moved, dancing around his fingers in search of refuge, perhaps seeking a path to freedom. He nudged it away, watching it disappear into a jungle of grass and weeds. He paused for a time, pensive yet alert.

Standing, he made an imprint, pressing down hard on the mud. As child-like as it was, he felt the urge to make his mark on the new world which his ancestors spoke of so highly. '*My first time on Earth,*' he thought jubilantly, '*perhaps the last...*' Knowing he had only a week, as Earth legislation permitted, he wanted to make the most of his experience. It would be another year before he could make the next trip. A deafening beep distracted him, dissolving his thoughts in an instant. He turned, gazing at a row of sky-cabs, the drivers in their matching blue uniforms and hats perspiring in the humidity of the day. Suddenly, a large group of tourists appeared, rushing out of the station, lugging bulky cases, rapidly dispersing in all directions.

Fishing deep inside his pockets with anxious hands, he pulled out his accommodation voucher, the one that came with the package deal. Small glossy and polished, it reflected the sunlight into his left eye. Across the voucher imprinted in black, were the words, '*Welcome to Earth...*'

After a smooth brisk air journey, the cab manoeuvred for descent, landing outside the Volux Hotel, its ten-star sign flashing and revolving every four seconds sequentially. Raising his hand before the code reader, the driver said, correctly, stiffly, "You're a Lunar resident, aren't you?"

"Yes, indeed I am. How did you perceive that? My clothes, no doubt."

The driver pointed to the small credit screen.

"No Earth resident gets charged that kind of tariff. Have a good day Sir."

Sean acknowledged the amount with disinterest, quickly shifting his glance towards the towering hotel. The cab door, via automatic control, slid open, concealing itself within its shell. He stepped out, regulating the temperature of his suit, his bag hanging across his shoulder loosely. Again he refocused and was taken aback by its stupendous design. It had the flair of an ancient Greek monument, carved and shaped to precision, an echo of the past. As he entered through the parting glass doors, a porter walked over.

"Welcome to the Volux Hotel. Please make your way to reception."

Sean commenced a slow walk over, and in the background captured muffled notes of hostility. People turned staring, hard and cold, child and adult alike. Their transparent resentment induced feelings of inadequacy within him, as if he were an invader from another world passing the outer limits. Accommodating himself to the ever-growing intimidating atmosphere, he reached the well-lit reception desk.

"Hello Sir," a tall, green-eyed lady said, her words spaced apart, her Russian accent dominant and penetrating.

"You're from Lunar aren't you Mr Winters?" She smiled, a smile that lit up her Slavic features, even teeth sparkling white under the intense overhead light.

"Yes, yes, I am. How did you know my name?"

"We have a tracking device implanted in the wall above. Within seconds it picks up all your data from your coded hand displaying it across my com-screen."

He grinned rubbing his chin.

"Tell me Mr Winters, I've always wondered what it must be like up there on the Moon. Haven't saved enough to get a flight yet... At night I often sit back and watch it, the near side of course. Because of the Moon's synchronous rotation, the far side is never visible."

"It's interesting, a totally different world even though it's so near. Sometimes it's the places closest to us that we take for granted. Man has a tendency to look afar. For an earth citizen it would be hard to adjust to a radically different social order."

Absorbed in his words for a time, she spoke. "I remember as a child seeing ships departing for Lunar on the vision-set." Her eyes now semi-closed, became distant as she reflected." They would take-off, leaving Terra, voyaging into space lining up with the Moon, falling into an orbit around it a hundred miles above its surface, guided down by magnetic controls but of course with anti-gravity technology it's all changed, if you can afford it."

Somewhat startled by her baffling fount of knowledge, he replied, "You seem pretty clued up for a receptionist. Sounds like you are speaking from personal experience."

"My dad was a Project Manager. He designed most of the ships for Lunar Voyagers. He would always go on about it."

With a warm waving motion of her hand, she now signalled over to a porter.

"You're all done Mr Winters."

"That's it?"

"Yes Sir, the machine above has obtained a photographic record of all your data, checking you in. To gain access to your room, simply pass your hand by the small blue code beam beside the door."

"Great, thanks."

Directed by the porter, he was led to his room on the fortieth floor. Sean flung his hand at the code beam. Magnetic locks instantly gave, slipping out of place. Then with a sharp click the door opened, swinging aside.

"Will that be all Mr Winters?"

"Yes, thank you."

"Sir, before I forget, we have a new service available for all our outer space guests. It's only just come in."

"Oh yeah?" Sean exclaimed attentively.

"It's a Virtual Chamber. In a few hours you can travel and see the world and all its beauty as if you were really there. You won't know the difference."

"Really?"

"Yes Sir, it's a very special machine," he said coaxingly. "If you require more information just dial 8 from your vidphone, you'll be put straight through."

Sean entered the room, its colour-alternating walls faintly luminous. Against the glass frame on a hanging picture, an angry fly buzzed. Dropping his bag onto the floor he walked over to the balcony, the doors sliding apart as the heat sensors registered. He stepped out stretching, gazing at the sun as it hung high above the face of the Atlantic. Then an intercity cruiser shot past, leaving a slash of billowing smoke in the atmosphere. Suddenly a thought struck him. '*This chamber... What was behind such a mechanism, how could it create such an illusion?*' A devouring curiosity grew within him. He stopped his introspection and headed inside. Now, beside the vidphone, he dialled 8, acquiring immediate connection.

"For visual transmission, press 1, if not please hold."

He refrained, opting for sound only. After a sequence of beeps a blade-sharp voice spoke.

"Erica Holmes, how can I assist you?"

"Yes hi, I'm interested in this Virtual Chamber."

"Oh yes, Sir," she replied brightly, "It's the latest machine, the very finest technology. At your own discretion and speed you can visit the world, all four corners of it: an experience of a lifetime. The procedure is simple, via vocal activation you can be anywhere you choose, and I mean anywhere... Asia, Africa, Europe... your choice."

There was a brief interval of silence.

"You see Sir, travelling with the Virtual Chamber is safer and easier, not to mention cost effective. Just think, in the legal week that you have as a Lunar resident you could never see the world in its entirety, not to mention the number of credits you would have to spend. But with the Virtual Chamber you can accomplish your wildest dreams within a matter of hours."

He interjected.

"How real does it feel, I mean I was told it's as if I were really there?"

"Yes Sir, that's correct. Your conscious mind won't know the difference. You will feel and see everything as if you were really there, as if you were part of that existence, that reality. One minute you'll be strolling through the city of Cairo, the next trudging through the jungles of Africa. It really is something phenomenal."

His face lit up with exuberance... pictures forming, weaving through his mind. The lady continued.

"And you can benefit further from the experience."

"How, in what way?"

"Photos can be included with the package to add verisimilitude to the journey, an extra touch of reality."

"Okay, so what's the total cost?" Sean inquired, his voice momentarily losing its spark.

"Eight hundred credits for an eight-hour journey. That's with everything included."

"Done," he said nodding in agreement, his expression set and assured.

"Great, as you are a guest, the V Chamber is available for you this evening. It operates on a twenty-four-hour basis, seven days a week and for your information, you are advised to stay away from alcohol."

"Tell me, what section of the hotel are you located in?"

He tapped his mouth with his fingers gently.

"Level thirty and if you require further information, just select X across your vision-set, it will give you a scientific breakdown of its function and will answer any niggling questions you may feel are of importance."

With a click, the call ended. Then, through a thin opening across the vid-phone unit, a note slithered out face down. Snatching it, he read.

"Thank you for your call, Mr Winters, the Volux Hotel wishes you a pleasant stay."

Sean sat on the bed, swiftly assimilating all the information. If only Lunar could have these machines, it would save so much credit and time, but in retrospect he knew it would never happen. The government would never implement the necessary legislation for the acquisition of such a machine. Solar travel would die... Lunar depended on it. He began to recollect the words which played in his mind... '*With the Virtual Chamber you can accomplish your wildest dreams...*' "Dreams being the operative word," he suddenly snapped bitterly. After all, however authentic it felt, virtual it remained, at least objectively. No matter what, the machine could never compare to the real thing, he concluded. In his mind it remained an ignominious option, but in the prevailing circumstances, a good one.

Striding lithely into the bathroom, he filled the sink with tepid water, splashing it across his face and neck. Although clearly exhausted and in need of sleep, the excitement of the moment kept him sharp and alert. He was filled with gleeful anticipation, unable to rest. Drying himself with a warm towel, he looked into the mirror, wondering what awaited him.

As evening approached, Sean walked out of the glass hover-lift, gazing back at the Moon nostalgically with a sense of awe. It was the first time he had seen it from another world, hanging there, suspended in the far-off distance, frozen in deep space, foggy webs of moisture drifting across its face. Memories flooded his mind, he recalled the times he would sit staring at the Earth from Lunar, wondering, thinking about the affinity between the two. After all, the Moon was responsible for most of the tidal effects seen on the Earth. Shrugging his shoulders, the metal lift doors closed, killing the scene.

Strolling down a long twisting hallway, luxury suites either side, he saw a flashing green sign. It read, 'V CHAMBER. GLOBAL TOUR.' In the background, he detected the enchanting chords of Far Eastern music, dimly echoing. As he reached the end of the hall, a vertically lifting door opened before him. He stepped in. Sean's attention was immediately drawn to a jet-black machine, its large frame occupying most of the space in the room. The V Chamber! It certainly resembled the images he had seen on the vision-set, but in reality, it had more to it, much more. It was spherical in shape, yet its middle section extended out, swollen, as if a ring had been placed around it.

Suddenly, he was approached by a tall athletic looking man, with short blond hair. Using his anthropological knowledge, Sean attempted to pinpoint his roots. Although Teutonic in appearance his slit eyes indicated an additional ethnic mix.

"Welcome Mr Winters, I'm Jessie, we've been expecting you."

He extended his hand in greeting. They shook.

"So Mr Winters, do you need me to go over anything?"

"No I'm all set," he said glancing at the V Chamber in bewildered wonder.

"Good, once you're strapped in, the computer will navigate you accordingly. It's straight forward."

In the moments of silence that followed, the machine started to drone, and its door slid open releasing a gush of vapour that instantly dissipated. Sean bit his lips in excitement. He could hear the sound of waking electronic components, which evidently controlled and operated the machine. As he entered, it lit internally, vividly displaying its slick design, and the glittering metal floor, an artefact of highly sophisticated technology. Above him, a recessed device took a beta-wave shot of his brain; an electric-eye.

"Journey well Sir, you have eight hours of pure pleasure."

Sean turned and waved as if actually believing he was about to embark on a global tour...a journey of a lifetime. After all it was nothing more than artificial construct, however convincing. The machine itself was partly responsible as it created an aura of its own. Inside, a blank screen encircled him three hundred and sixty degrees. Monitors and machines flickered beneath, bleeping and humming, a whole combination of computerized activity. He dropped into a white chair located in the centre of the chamber and a strap automatically latched itself around him, securing and bolting itself into the floor. Above his head, supported by a thin silver wire, a mask descended, halting as it reached his lap. Then a piercing female voice spoke, as cold ventilated air began pouring in beneath him.

"Welcome Mr Winters. Please secure the mask onto your face."

Rapidly he fitted it, his eyes now staring from beyond the glass view plate of the mask. Again, the electric-eye took a wave shot of his brain. It registered, storing the data, displaying it across a luminous screen which ejected from the floor in front of him. Eric was now falling into relax mode; this progressive mood change was detected, his brainwaves switching from alpha to theta, higher amplitude lower frequency.

Outside, a technician made final checks, using a reference sheet as his guide. A small component was then inserted into an aperture located to the back of the machine. It fitted perfectly, moulded symmetrically to the precise dimensions of the opening. The V Chamber burst into life with a series of lateral oscillations, lifting into a fixed position above the ground, a metre high. It hung there stationary, defying the laws of gravity. Slowly it began to rotate gathering velocity, until it reached its set speed. Inside, Sean sat calm and focused, unaware and unaffected by its motion. Suddenly the lighting faded into complete darkness, contrary to the tubular screen which now flashed into activity. Displayed across it, was a list of destinations.

"Please select," the voice instructed him.

The chair in which he sat began to revolve, slow but constant. Arm locks folded automatically. Contemplating the list, he thought, '*Africa... I've heard so much about its natural beauty... Mountains... Mount Kilimanjaro, three degrees South of the Equator.*' He was flooded with awe and reverence. "Africa," he rasped energetically. "Kilimanjaro..."

Within a fraction of a second, as if space, time, and matter had collapsed around him, the raw material of the physical world, he was transported via computerized deception through a dark vacuum. An unyielding darkness replaced everything, sealing him away from reality. Then light, golden sunlight shone around him through thin parting clouds above the shimmering landscape of Tanzania. "I'm here," he said prodding himself, as if for confirmation. He could even detect the faint odours that lingered from the rain drenched forests, captivating him as he inhaled each and every scent.

Beneath him, he could feel the soil and undergrowth as he moved his feet in varied directions. Then he saw Kilimanjaro soaring high, penetrating the atmosphere. In the distance, people and animals roamed alike, faint but definite images of life. His face dripped in sun inflicted perspiration, drops of salty moisture irritating his eyes. '*Amazing*,' he thought, even his body responded chemically to the environment as if he were really there. For the first time he knew what it really felt like to be a part of earthly reality, as if he had been reconnected to the flow of life and time. Away from it was emptiness, darkness, nothing but an indoor world comprised of man-made structures in order to generate a Terra-like environment, but even then, nothing like this. This was home, this is where man belonged. Overhead, birds hovered, chirping sounds of communication, darting back and forth, insects buzzing, tiny specks of life, splendour and beauty everywhere; life, life in abundance. Refocusing, he viewed the giant stratovolcano for the last time. With another destination in mind, he said, "Brazil, the Amazon."

In a flash the scene blurred, swirling away from him in a vortex, with it his sensations and emotions. Again darkness replaced everything, then the light returned. He now stood engulfed by tall trees, sunlight partially filtering through. In the background he captured echoes, echoes that signified life, the dominance of nature. Bending, he saw a coiled gleaming snake. He studied its deadly design. It seemed unaware of his existence, its tiny eyes devoid of any spark or awareness. He recalled that its lethal venom was a complex mixture of proteins and enzymes but of course it posed no threat, after all it was just a computerized illusion.

He stood calmly, the weight of his feet seeming to crush the endless carpet of green leaves and undergrowth. The air was bug infested, thick and moist, filled with the odour of plants and fetid rot. Across his legs insects crawled, countless kinds, tiny insignificant yet complex organic life. He trudged on through the wild steaming jungle. Around him, shapes moved; vines and leaves dripping with wet slime.

His clothes and face were now saturated in sticky sweat, a result of the scorching heat and stifling humidity. A jaguar appeared from out of nowhere, its golden reddish-brown eyes alive and roaming. The powerful animal prowled in search of prey. Although rigidly conscious of the pseudo environment, Sean froze, his heart constricted, rapidly retrieving its rhythm; metabolic secretions of fear working inside his body. Repressing the thalamic impulses he recaptured his composure, reminding himself that it was a plastic reality. But what if it attacked, would it leave inauthentic wounds, scars? Just how real was it all?

Now calm and eager, he gazed upon it, admiring its structure and beauty, staring hard at its tawny yellow fur, which was marked with dark spots, clusters of them. '*Its design was too elaborate and perfect to be the product of mere chance,*' he thought. Lunar was governed by an atheistic philosophy, one which he had questioned countless times. Although via powerful telescope he had captured vague images of Earth life, being a part of it was totally different, even though virtual.

Satisfied he moved on feverishly, pushing past a wall of green growth, creepers lodged inside; an elaborate selection buzzing with life. Absorbing as much as the eye could see, he now had the urge for an underwater experience. '*The ocean...! What must it be like beneath it?*' he thought. Summoning courage he yelled, "The Pacific waters, the Great Barrier Reef!"

Again, the scene vanished, light and life dissolving before him... As darkness parted, he found himself beneath the deep. Instantly, he realised he could breathe without the aid of canned air, the one flaw in such a convincing fabricated illusion. The warm blue crystal waters thrived with symbiotic life of all kinds, shapes and sizes, some transparent, glowing, pulsating with brilliant alternating colours and bioluminescence. Beneath him, fixed to the sea floor lay colourful corals; skeletal remains of marine organisms from the class Anthozoa. From the corner of his eye, he saw a giant yet docile manta ray, gliding gracefully towards him, its skin deceptively smooth.

As it swept past it seemed to enjoy human interaction, responding to Sean's subtle hand signals. Then, he spotted a dolphin, an aquatic mammal, its streamlined fusiform body and distinct beak marking it out from the large fish which encircled it. Again, Sean digested the scene, somewhat philosophically, somewhat passionately. *'Nature, what was the force behind it, what held all things together?'* With a series of forward strokes he moved ahead, awed by the engulfing splendour. Even in the deepest depths of Terra, life dwelled. He could now see all kinds of marine life; stone fish, sharks, sea snakes, jellyfish, but one creature in particular amazed him, one he had heard about, in mythological dialogue, an octopus. Via jet propulsion it would move rapidly, uniquely, in contrast to the other species. Sean's face lit with awe as he gazed at its tentacles. *'What an intricate looking creature, what a complex nervous system it must have.'* He marvelled further as it darted away into the blue.

Having quenched his desire for an underwater experience, he called out, "Japan, Tokyo." For some obscure reason he felt the need, a sudden impulse. The sound transmission from his voice catapulted him to yet another destination. Sean now stood on a busy high street, cloud penetrating buildings all around, oriental people rushing in varied directions, young and old alike, beautiful stomach-churning aromas assailing his nostrils. Overhead, sky-vehicles hovered, others disappearing beyond the line of the horizon at daring speeds. Stepping from the walkway he crossed the road, impeding mid-afternoon traffic.

Horns beeped, voices rose yelling in a foreign tongue. As he reached the other side, he halted, gazing at a neatly clipped tree swaying in the breeze. A magnificent building then caught his attention, one which was able to transform itself into a series of elaborate shapes according to temperature change. To his surprise, an old Japanese man walked over, dressed in a luminous yellow outfit, his face filled with lines of age, his eyes deep-set, blazing with energy, full of expression... '*So much for illusion*,' he thought. Although he strolled past him without any interaction, the man appeared excited by his presence. Sean sat resting his heels on the pavement. He moistened his lips, rubbing his chin. '*Where else*,' he pondered, '*where to next?*'

The scenes continued to appear at his command, beautiful landscapes, various destinations, virtual but real, at least real to him, a subjective reality, one which satisfied him fully. Suddenly, there was a flash of intense light which snapped him away from the clutches of the plastic world. Opening his eyes he found himself sitting motionless, staring towards the tubular screen, lit and active, pulsing but blank, mask across his face, streaked with lines of sweat.

"Thank you for journeying with the Virtual Chamber. We look forward to having you aboard again soon."

He pulled off the mask and the belt automatically released itself, sliding back into the chair for concealment. Again, thoughts began to race through his mind. *'How could Lunar and its governing bodies teach atheism? How could they feed people this mathematically illogical philosophy? All things in space and time, every single particle, atom, had to have an origin, surely? Even the planets which revolved around the life bearing sun were all purposely positioned, spinning at a controlled velocity which allowed life to exist on Earth. Everything throughout the universe is finely balanced, working in symbiosis, equilibrium. If only the people of Lunar had more freedom to journey to Earth on a regular basis, they would see its spectacular design and all the life forms that flourish in it, something Lunar was devoid of. Powerful telescopes were not enough to convey the right message the message that Earth was so very special and that the fabricated worlds elsewhere in the solar system were nothing in comparison to that of this planet. Observation from a distance could never compare. To be a part of earthly existence opened up a whole new way of thinking, about life, the world, the universe, and more importantly our place in it.'*

Heading for the door, it slid open. Calmly, he stepped out and was instantly in contact with a rep, this time a young lady, who beamed at him warmly.

"Mr Winters how was your trip?"

"Amazing… No words to describe it. It certainly vindicated the words of the lady who sold me the package, but it's now time for the real thing. I have six days left here... need to sightsee as much as possible."

"Indeed, New York has many attractions. It even has the first underwater resort, only five miles out across the Atlantic."

He smiled, recalling his experience, his eyes philosophical and bright. '*As beautiful as it was, the real thing has to be better...*'

The Man Who Awoke Yesterday

Provoked by a sense of doom, Dirk Allen awoke. Hungover and with semi-closed eyes, he could detect, almost smell, the unfamiliarity of his surroundings. Leaping from the bed in his creased grey suit, he was immediately struck by the crushing fact that his room was no more. Instead he now stood in a luscious apartment, the glazed marble floor dimly reflecting his image. With a trail of clues, the one question remained, where was he? His intuition told him nothing, his anxiety grew as he began to recollect the night past, scrutinizing each and every moment. *'A few drinks downtown... a cab, then home. What about that blonde chick at the bar? No, I never ended up going back to her place.'* He scratched his chin, head down, eyes on the floor. The whole weird experience was enough to penetrate his alcoholic haze, which was now rapidly fading.

Beyond the door there was motion, a rustling of keys commingling with the vocal chimes of happiness. As the door swung open a woman walked in, her svelte frame clothed in a pink dress, exposing most of her shapely thighs. Flinging off her high heels, she paused and shot him a glance.

"Good day Dirk," she said with a deep southern accent, her eyes bright blue, full of confidence and self-satisfaction.

"You're not bad looking at all... just as I specified."

A series of puzzled expressions flashed across his face. With a big teeth-exposing grin, she turned strolling barefoot into the adjoining kitchenette, her damp feet leaving faint imprints across the marble floor. Incensed by this chain of wacky events, he rushed over shaking his head.

"Look here lady, what's this all about?"

He began to twist and turn, absorbing the surroundings.

"Who are you anyway? How did I get here?"

"Dirk sweetheart," she replied. "Now that you are here with me nothing else in this universe should matter."

He frowned with a piercing silent stare. His eyes did not waver from her.

"Listen lady, I haven't time for games. I'm not following your drift."

"It's simple." She brushed back her blond locks. "You are, because I say you are."

For a brief moment he considered her words but could make nothing of them.

"Let's start again." He shook his head.

"Dirk, you're just not understanding me, are you?"

She eyed him intently, resting a hand on her hip.

"Let's put it like this... you are a construct of my mind. Today is your time to be a part of my world, a part of my existence."

"Sure," he muttered acidly, "I get it, you're the local fruitcake, I just happened to run into, right? Sorry lady, it's time for me to rejoin the real world!"

"Dirk!"

Turning to go, he froze, his legs stiffening into immobility, as if the woman's voice held some kind of magnetic property. Although he felt in control, he didn't move.

"Sweetheart, you're not the first guy to react like this, and certainly not the last."

Motionless, he listened, backing down lamely, his face pale and drawn.

"Out there you're nothing without me whether you like it or not. You can't just pick up and leave."

"So what are you suggesting then?"

"Just that."

Her eyes rolled amorously, her long dark lashes fluttering. Enraged by her dismissive care-free attitude, he raised his hand pointing at her, breaking free from his hypnotic daze.

"That does it. I'm out of here."

Hurrying to the door, he left, descending a flight of dusty stairs towards the exit below. Out on the busy Chicago sidewalk, Dirk moved sluggishly towards home mixing in with the flow of people and noise, hands deep inside his trouser pockets, shoulders sagging with fatigue. '*That half-crazed chick...! What was that all about? She was cute though. I must have been really out of it,*' he thought. Suddenly he thought of home. But where was it? Betrayed by his memory, he paused mystified, his features contorting as he pondered deeper, thinking at high speed. 'T*hat's it, how could I forget? Ellisville, Ellisville's home...*'

At the smog-filled train station, Dirk walked over to the ticket office, dollars in hand.

"Where to, Buddy?" the ticket clerk asked, puffing away at a cigar, his thinning hair hanging over his face and ears.

"Ellisville please."

"Where?"

"Ellisville."

"Never heard of it."

"What...!"

"You heard," the clerk said, regarding him sharply.

"Wait a minute. Are you telling me..."

"Yes, that's right. Now if you wouldn't mind, I have a line of people behind you waiting to buy tickets."

The clerk's voice was filled with frustration as he leaned on the counter, peering closely into his face. Dirk glanced over his shoulder at the long line of people. Men and women stood there alike, grumbling and rolling their eyes impatiently. Turning back to the ticket clerk, he said, "Look Mr, I've lived there most my life. There must be some kind of mistake."

The clerk's mouth opened and closed, but no sound came. Then he pointed at the half dangling chart board with a finger.

"Look, a list of all the stops, but no Ellisville... satisfied?

Dirk studied it anxiously, but it wasn't there. Not a trace of it, as if it had been wiped out of existence. From behind, he felt a cold hand tug at him.

"Hey, what's going on?" a middle-aged suited man complained, adjusting his glasses. "I've got to be at work in the next ten minutes."

He tapped his wrist at an imaginary watch. Clutching onto him with trembling hands Dirk spoke, his voice choking with emotion, "Sir perhaps you can help?"

The man eyed him up and down, switching his focus towards the clerk and back.

"Ellisville, you've heard of Ellisville... right?" Dirk's voice sank with desperate pleading hope.

"Never heard of it."

"But... but how can that be?"

The stabbing reality was too much to take in as it reached his conscious mind. Brutal, overt fear had taken over, distorting his features and stance, inner forces conspiring, working, pulling him emotionally apart. In an instant, Dirk released his grip on the man and darted away, almost losing his footing, the line of people turning and grumbling in bewildered annoyance.

Under dim lights, in a downtown bar, Dirk swept back his third shot of bourbon, gulping it down, his head moving to the melodic notes uttered from the jukebox in the corner. The alcohol had now taken effect as it rose up inside him, mildly suppressing his natural emotions and reactions. Then, sliding a quarter into a pay phone beside the bar, he dialled amidst a maze of empty beer bottles.

"Hello," a voice murmured groggily.

"Rita, please listen to me... just give me a second."

"Listen Mr, can you stop calling, this is the third time today. I don't know you... good day!"

The phone slammed down; Dirk's heart constricted, flooding his body with a cold tingling sensation, the dim lights concealing his fright filled features.

"Damn," he cried, banging his fist against the counter.

His mind suddenly went blank, as if he had lost his identity, and had become an inanimate object. His whole world was now in jeopardy. He recalled little, but even more bizarrely, no-one seemed to remember him or his little hometown of Ellisville. Who was he? What were these memories and past recollections he had? How could he trust them? That woman, who was she? What was she? Could it be he was a creation of someone's will, stepping through a series of windows into different times, dimensions... a metaphysical multiplexity of realities?

Across from him, in silence, the bar tender indicated another shot, making a drinking motion with his hand. In reply Dirk shook his head. Then from behind him, someone squeezed his arm. He turned, and there before him stood the unknown woman, dolled up, oozing with confidence and panache, beaming at him warmly.

"Hi gorgeous."

Dirk swallowed hard, and drew a breath, body tense.

"Who are you? What do you want from me?"

She smiled, teeth sparkling white in the half light. With her cold bony hand she began toying with the buttons of his shirt. With slow twisting motions, she unfastened one.

"You sweetheart... You wouldn't be here otherwise."

She leaned over to kiss him, lips pouting. Raising his hand he pushed her away.

"Stop talking in riddles," Dirk protested, his voice faltering, his breath reeking of alcohol.

"Dirk love, you must understand one thing."

She lit a cigarette, the tip glowing red as she took a steady puff, directing it into his face.

"All that you are is because of me and this is why you partially exist in this world of mine."

Choking, he waved his hand into the quickly fading smoke, his eyes semi-closed and red rimmed.

"Partially? You could have fooled me." He touched his face with both hands, as if examining; a sarcastic gesture to reinstate his existence.

"Dirk, you are really hard headed." She puffed again, marking the cigarette with her red lipstick.

"Don't you get it yet? Dirk Allen never existed, at least not here. Maybe in another universe, another time, you were a part of someone else's world, someone else's reality but here you are mine, solely mine."

There was a moment of silence, as if there was a hidden twisted truth in what she was saying. An inconceivable terrifying truth.

"I don't get it!"

"Don't try, you never will. Just enjoy your time while it lasts... at this rate it won't be very long."

"What's that supposed to mean?"

"Just as I willed you into existence," she lowered her gaze, smirking; a cold secret smirk, "I can, quite easily, will you out. Remember you're only a construct of my mind."

His eyes grew wide and envenomed.

"Do you really think I believe this garbage?" He yelled.

His voice increased in volume and confidence. Then, he reflected. The one undeniable problem which lingered deep inside him, was the fact she was the only thing that made him feel alive and real, nullifying that absurd inexplicable void within. It gave him hope, a sense of certainty, a sense of being, yet he refused to accept the necessity of her presence.

"What about..."

"Dirk," she said sharply, halting him midway through his sentence. "Don't talk about memories, they are yours... perhaps from another time and place but here they mean nothing."

"Hey, how did you know what I was going to say?"

"I've heard it a million times over. You're not the first and you won't be the last."

Stubbing out her cigarette against the counter, she dropped it to the floor grinding it down with her heel.

"Come on, let's go take a ride."

Pulling him by his crumpled grey jacket, she led him outside into the parking lot. There was a chill wind, sharp and penetrating, a line of trees swaying, bending furiously. The cold instantly roused him. Shakily, he crossed his arms pressing them against his chest. Above, the clouds dispersed, almost vanishing, leaving the skyline bare, unveiling the dim night spheres in the slowly growing gloom.

"Where are you taking me?"

"Dirk, you know something... you ask too many questions."

Walking over to a bright silver Mustang, she stepped in opening the passenger door.

"Hop in," she said coaxingly, starting the motor, revving the engine.

He stood at the door awkwardly, uncertain whether to enter, tempted purely by curiosity. The wind began nudging and biting into him, almost forcing him into the car, as if the elements had conspired to lure him into the clutches of the unknown woman.

"Come on sweetheart, this in our night, the first of many."

Grim faced he entered, gazing at her with opposing emotions. Turning, he looked ahead through the moisture-stained windscreen, feeling acutely helpless. What was next?

Down a wide city road, they moved swiftly, odometer racing, cars and motorbikes zooming past, tiny dark specks rushing through the evening twilight.

"Can you please tell me where we are going?"

"You know something? Of all the guys, you're the one who's really given me a hard time. Time is all you have, so enjoy it."

The glow and sparkle in her eyes began to diminish to a more serious and cynical look, almost cadaverous, as if all life had melted away within her. For a time there was silence, neither of them spoke. Tall grey streetlights suddenly activated, illuminating the city. Darkness had descended, pitch black. Ahead, he could see neon lights, green, red and blue, music pumping, vibrating and echoing, chaos everywhere. Clubs and bars filled the streets, row after row of night activity, youngsters swarming around chatting, mumbling meaningless sounds.

Pulling over, she yanked the brakes, killing the drive in an instant with a sickening jolt. Vigour for life had now returned to her.

"Come on, let's party."

A parking attendant walked up from beyond the restless crowds, tipping his cap.

"Sorry mam, this is a tow-away zone."

"But I can park here, right...?"

"Right, take as long as you like. Have a great night ma'am."

"What," Dirk gasped, astonished at the attendant's reaction.

Pushing through a long line, she walked up to the entrance of a club, Dirk following desperately behind, sweat trickling down his neck and into his collar. Without a word, two burly bouncers parted, revealing the elegant entrance. A gold-coloured carpet lay there, elaborate patterns woven into it.

"Have a wonderful night, ma'am," they muttered timidly, half bowing.

Dirk followed, puffing and red faced. Grabbing his arm, she steered him through the plush doors, towards the rhythmic rumble of sound and motion. In the middle of a small brown table an artificial candle burned. Facing each other, they sat in silence, throwing sporadic glances around the dance floor.

"Tell me Dirk, do you like dancing? I love the way people express their emotions, feelings, through different sounds." She rocked her head to the rackety beats.

"No," he snapped with a sudden flicker of aversion, his voice rising above the blaring music which sent faint vibrations across the table.

"Where would you like to live? I've always fancied Denver." For a brief moment she closed her eyes dreamily, crossing her legs. "Those beautiful mountains, all that fresh air... wooden cabin, oak fireplace..."

"Anywhere away from you would be ideal."

"Oh dear," she gasped. "What's wrong now?"

"You...! This, all this...!" He stood up nervously, waving his arms in the air, sitting moments later. "I can't believe I'm actually here listening to you."

His whole approach had now reversed. The cooperative attitude that had brought him this far had somehow reverted, acting like a catalyst, bringing back those negative emotions in him. He was caught in a cycle of negativity. Yet in the back of his mind, unanswered questions roamed plucking at him every now and then. Ellisville... his vague memories of it... this lady, his gut feelings... Where would he go from here? '*Away from her, away from her would be a start*,' he thought.

"Dirk, I'm beginning to realise we are not meant for each other."

"No kidding lady."

"I don't think you understand. Without me you cease to be. This is my world; an entire world revolving around me."

A waiter walked over, his eyes bright in the candlelight.

"Drinks?"

She shook her head signalling no, then indicated five minutes with her bony hand.

"Tell me, what makes you believe that this world is yours?"

"That's just how it is; that's just how it has always been. You are a part of it because I willed you into being. The only real living thing in this world is me. All that you see is only partially real."

"So I don't exist? In fact, no one does but you right?"

"Kind of..."

"So if this is your world, and you can have anything you want, why is it from the very moment we met, I've been trying to avoid you?"

"True love has to come naturally; it can't be forced. I've given you that wonderful gift, free will. Choose wisely." She smiled a cold humourless smile.

"This has gone far enough. Theoretically speaking, am I to believe I'm some lingering, partial existent entity surrounded by an illusionary world of your creation?"

"Theoretically," she replied, her voice tinged with patronizing overtones.

"Right, that's it. No more games. It ends here."

Dirk leapt up and darted towards the exit, barging past a crowd of drunkards, the woman following closely behind. Out in the cold night, the city streets were almost bare.

"Dirk, do you realise what this means? I don't think you do."

He halted and turned.

"Yes, yes in fact I do. You and I finish here. Read my lips." He pointed at his mouth. "Goodbye... Oh, just one thing before I go. Purely out of curiosity, what is your name?"

"What does it matter now? You and I ain't meant to be...
right Dirk?"

"Right..." He shook his head; his cheeks flushed red with
indignation. 'I can't believe I've played along with this,'
he thought.

He walked off hunched over, entering a dark bare section
of the city. Nothing moved. Detecting faint clattering
footsteps he turned spotting her in the moonlight, the
wind whistling around him.

"You still ain't getting it are you? I'm out of here."

In the blink of an eye, Dirk puffed out of existence. All
that remained where he stood was a smoky haze which
quickly faded, dissipating into the void. Gazing at the
empty space he had occupied, she turned and began
strolling back to the car, a circle of light engulfing her.
No matter how long she waited, she was bound to get
it right sometime. The right one had to come sooner or
later."

Slit in the Sky

"Professor Western, are you certain that all earth life originated from aliens?"

The cam-crew focused in, lights from the studio shining towards him. He smiled, eyes fixed and arrogant, beaming with reflected glory.

"Yes...yes indeed I am."

He adjusted his necktie, his chest swelling with pride.

"In recent years it has been only a plausible theory, a hypothesis to be exact, but now, as we speak, it's absolute fact."

The audience sat in stunned silence, the host referring to his digital-note-screen.

"But how Mr Western, how can you be certain? What tangible evidence do you have?"

Slowly the images began to fade, and now in a daze of timeless half sleep he awoke, the ceiling jet vent spraying him with a morning dose of bacterial repellent. Instantly he registered reality, detecting movement, as the auto-coffee maker wheeled itself towards the bed, halting in the half shadow of the room. After languidly sipping a cup, he washed, changed, and was then ready for his appointment with the Atlantic City Times with just five minutes to spare. Darting down the stairs to his study, he stepped into his newly invented Trans-propeller, a tall, narrow, metallic unit, its interior gleaming wickedly with lights, knobs and switches of all kinds.

"Eric darling," rasped the nagging voice of his wife. "What time will you be back?"

"As soon as I'm done..."

"Thank goodness you've got a unit installed back at the office. It was taking you hours to get back home through the busy commercial lanes, that endless tide of traffic."

She walked into the study stirring a cup of nutra-vite mineral drink, its foul odour mixing with the scent of his cologne.

"Tina, I wish you'd stop drinking that. The only way you'll ever lose weight is if you stop eating," he barked, rolling his eyes away from her, back to the monitor, his face ablaze with technological know-how.

Dismissively, stubbornly, she replied, "How long will it be before the T-propeller is sold commercially?"

"That's for the government to decide. It won't be easy to stop all air-cruisers and surface-vehicles... too many credits involved. It's highly political." He shook his head in annoyance. Then, turning a dial with careful deliberation he was gone in a flash, the unit vibrating faintly, glowing dimly red.

Eric reappeared at his office, beside another T-propeller, a slightly modified version, in contrast to the one back home. It was bigger, more spacious and elaborate. Adjusting his tie he sat at his desk, peering out of the window, contemplating the scene. Air-cruisers were landing in swarms, roads choked with traffic and people dashing to work. Calmly he lit a cigar, leaning back. It flared, burning red hot, infesting the room with smoke. He sucked in expertly, puffing out, pride and achievement etched into his features. He had started the day exactly right, fresh and unfazed as always. There was a knock at the door, then another, a frightened repetitive tap.

"Come in Wendy," he snapped, recognising the distinctive knock. The cute-faced receptionist turned the handle, popping her head around the door, blushing sweetly.

"Professor, Mr Coin from the ACT Newspaper is here to see you."

"Great! Bring him through."

He stubbed out his cigar in the hydro-tray, sitting upright, professional. A rugged looking man stumbled in, briefcase in one hand, hanky in the other. He was dressed in a creased blue suit, his shirt collar loose and open, a black tie hanging from it.

"James Coin, ACT."

They shook… a tight firm shake.

James felt a little flustered at meeting such an eminent man but pulled himself together.

"Professor Western… delighted to meet you."

The name thundered in his ears creating ripples of awe. He was trying to project a cool, calm, professional demeanour but he could not help himself.

"I can't believe it. I'm standing in front of history. Is it really you, the greatest pioneer since Walter Stevenson?"

Eric nodded with a smile.

"Please Mr Coin, take a seat."

He indicated the chair on the opposite side of the desk.

"Tell me, just curious... Were you always fascinated with machines... as a kid I mean?"

"Yes, I was. My father once told me that man is a machine maker, constructing greater and more complex working elements. From that day on, I developed an interest."

"Okay, so to today's business... As you know I'm here about your invention. The...." He paused.

"T-propeller," Eric said in a low modulated voice, pointing towards it. James' eyes followed his hand, his face slightly flushed with relief.

"That's it. Keep forgetting the name," he said in stunned admiration. "Wow, it looks even more complex than the photos portray."

He turned to face Eric.

"You've made history Professor. Citizens all over the US and overseas have been raving about it. Now tell me, give me a brief run down on how it operates... its benefits."

He opened his briefcase, pulling out his digi.

"With all due respect, the mathematical formula is unique and strictly confidential. There are things I would rather keep private even then the explanation would be far too mind-boggling for you to grasp. With regard to its benefits, well that's self-evident, is it not?"

"Yes but I'd appreciate it if we could get your own words on this please," James said as he activated the registering vocalizer.

Eric got up, pacing around the room, hands behind his back.

"The T-propeller was designed to catapult a person or object to a set destination anywhere on the globe, to the specific location of your choice by the use of an intricate co-ordinate mechanism and hopefully soon, we will extend it to other parts of our solar system and galaxy, planets that are well known holiday destinations, like Mars, with no time lapse, consequently revolutionizing space travel and indeed all forms of travel as we know it."

"Mars...! That's great Professor. I have relatives there. The sooner, the better. I hate the journey. But you mention the word hopefully. Why?"

"At present I have no proof that it can work outside of this planet. It still needs to be tested, but I am certain it will. To summarise, there will be no need for air-cruisers or surface- vehicles, here on Earth. They will be a thing of the past."

James checked the digi as the words the professor had just uttered danced across the screen, the vocalizer working efficiently and rapidly.

"Please continue."

"I have almost a 70-mile trek from home to work... it took me less than a second... no headaches, no sky or road traffic, no stress or speeding tickets and there will be no excuses from late employees once it is commercially on the market of course!"

James smiled in amusement. "You were last quoted, only a few weeks back, saying that the device operates by bridging distances, non-spatially through," he cut off to check his notes... "through another dimension, correct?"

"I've already made it clear once, Mr Coin." The professor raised his hand to emphasise the point. "I will not disclose any more information on technical methods or go into the physics of it for that matter."

"Fine, but please, hear me out."

Eric halted, peering down at him.

"During that brief second of launch where do you go? You must go somewhere! When on the market, buyers will demand to know and you as manufacturer will be forced to answer... I'd like a factual answer, please Professor."

"Okay fine," Eric said with reluctance, now sitting, leaning back against his flexible chair, legs crossed.

"Let's just say you are catapulted into another dimension. Out of this continuum..."

The digi registered with a series of clicks.

"How many units have you built to date?"

"Ten. Eight are kept back at the workshop... the other two I use myself... one here, one at home."

"Any initial defects?"

"Would I be looking to put it on the market if there were? No, of course not," he bristled indignantly, and James made a mental note to dial back his tone a bit as the professor continued...

"My two technicians and I went through thousands of vigorous tests… no failures… no defects. We even formulated a list of dates for periodic inspection."

"How long do you estimate it will be before it is sold to the general public?"

"Can't answer that right now, the political implications are vast. The problem is this invention could destabilise society. Businesses will collapse worldwide, ones like EPO and Jefferson Engineering. Companies that are responsible for constructing surface-vehicles and air-cruisers will all go bust and many others will inevitably follow. It's just not as easy as you think. It's a major leap from what we are used to, a total transition. There has to be time for adjustment, time for the major change. The travel and transport industry will totally die because of my invention. Only I, as creator, designer and manufacturer of the T-propeller can legally use one at present and enjoy all its benefits… but due to my altruistic tendencies, I hope that will soon change."

'*This has him really worried*,' thought James, '*maybe that's where his arrogance is coming from. It's defensive*.' He moved on to his next question.

"Any drawbacks with the unit?"

"One! An obvious one."

"Which is?" James asked, somewhat surprised by his reply.

"In order to travel back to the point of launch in the same manner wherever it may be, you would need another unit at your destination. Like me for example, one unit here, one at home."

"So what you're saying is if I travelled to Mars with the T-propeller, I would need another unit there in order to get back the same way I got there."

"Exactly..."

The phone-com rattled across the desk, breaking the flow of the discussion. Turning a dial Eric terminated the call.

An interval of silence passed...

"Now my friend, it's time to reveal something to you... something I haven't shared with anyone."

'*Here we go*,' thought James leaning forward slightly in anticipation. "Please continue Professor."

"I'm planning to attempt a journey beyond our galaxy... beyond what we know, using the T-propeller."

"But you said it still needs to be tested and that's in relation to our solar system... our galaxy. But why..."

Eric interjected.

"James, if I can prove it works in our solar system and indeed our galaxy there's no reason to believe it won't work outside of it. In terms of getting back to Earth, I will bring a large box with me with all the essential parts and mechanisms so that I can build the return T-propeller, that way I can return safely home to Earth. Now, I'm targeting the galaxy Andromeda. I've been planning it, studying it, even dreaming of it."

"But why journey to other parts of the universe where nothing exists or at least there is no certainty of any life?"

"My friend, my mission has solely one purpose, to prove that alien life exists. I have a theory that life on Earth was created by extraterrestrials. To prove this to myself, and the world, would mean having to go there."

"Okay, but where exactly is Andromeda?" James asked.

"Nearby, relatively speaking of course... 2.2 million light years away. A place beyond, a leap into the unknown. Naturally I would have to target one specific planet within the galaxy, making all the correct calculations. It's a journey I feel compelled to take, whatever the consequences, life or death."

"But, but what are the odds of finding aliens there? I mean it's such a gamble, and after all, none have been seen in our galaxy. What makes you believe you'll find them elsewhere? What concrete evidence do you have?"

"None, but I do have an old book, written by a very famous Astrophysicist, Henry Wicks, who claims to have been visited by aliens from the galaxy Andromeda. He was told no other race of aliens existed, other than theirs, and that their race inhabited every single planet within their galaxy, and that they all originated from the planet Ius. This makes my job a lot easier. All I need do is choose one planet."

"So in short, you are prepared to journey into the depths of the universe to prove that nothing else is responsible for creating life on Earth, other than these aliens mentioned in an old book, even at the potential cost of your life, with no tangible evidence of their existence other than a theory, and the words of a man?"

"Correct. In essence, I'm a modern-day Christopher Columbus. He crossed the vast expanse of the Atlantic with a dream. I'll journey into the emptiness of space with another, only mine is a far bigger challenge to say the least."

"Well," James said sitting back and watching the Professor's face carefully for a minute, looking for any sign that he was having his leg pulled. The guy seemed totally serious and what's more, projected an absolute faith in what he was saying. James had a thousand more questions to ask but he decided to end the interview there. He was almost convinced this was real and he did not want to alienate the Professor at this stage. Chances were the scoop would be his when the time came, if he managed things right now. With a swift motion of his hand, James deactivated the digi. He then placed the digi in his briefcase.

"I guess that wraps things up." He got up. "Thank you for your time professor. I'll have the credits sent through to your account within the hour. We'll be in touch and good luck."

He reached out a moist palm and they shook, a delighted, friendly shake.

James walked out, closing the door behind him. For a moment Eric wondered why he had ended the interview so abruptly. Had something he'd said triggered the journalists prompt exit, or was it just him, his usual bout of crazed paranoia. Consulting his table clock he decided, that was that. Raising the phone-com, he pressed a button and was put through with visual transmission. He could see his wife in the bathroom humming, singing and splashing, bare and pink under a steaming hot shower.

"Hi honey," she cried out piercingly in an attempt to speak over the sound of the running water. "Are you coming home?"

Across the screen the images soon became cloudy, as the quickly forming moisture partially masked the view.

"Yes, be there in approximately three minutes."

"Okay, I'll go prepare you a snack... your favourite sandwich."

"Great."

He watched as she stepped out of the shower, lifting a blue towel from the floor with the aid of her toe. Wrapping the warm fabric around her she smiled and waved. He disconnected and the scenes vanished. Arranging the phone-com into its usual position, he rasped, "Wendy." There was movement, heels tapping against the floor. The door opened.

"Yes."

"I'm off. Take all messages for me, or rather, re-circulate them to my home number, if urgent. See you in the morning."

"Okay Professor."

Rising from his chair he walked over and entered the T-propeller through the revolving doors. Above his head, lights and bulbs glowed, periodically, sequentially. Gazing at the control board, his fingers flew, and in a flash he was gone, faster than light.

Eric reappeared in what looked like a hazy, grey, tubular tunnel. Immediately, without panicking, he realised he had somehow been caught between his world and the other, trapped in a bubble between reality and the other dimension as he had explained it. The tunnel stretched like a pipe with no visible end. There was no sound or motion, other than the audible beating of his heart. The whole experience had a dreamlike, sluggish quality to it.

With measured steps he began to walk. The ground beneath him was real, substantial, his footsteps even echoed faintly. He was engulfed by awe, nullifying all his natural emotions and biological instincts... fear, desperation, worry, doom... His features were twisting in a strange excitement, trance-like in overwhelming disbelief. As he reached the end, there was no cut off point as such, no barrier or wall, just a luminous glaze, and something inside it moved. Approaching it face on, he bent slowly. Amazingly his office came into view.

It was presented to him as if watching it from a small circular vision-screen, yet the image was indistinct, blurry, milky, wavering, and from it no sound came. He could see his mahogany desk and chair, his library of books, atlas globe and fishing rods, even his portrait hanging on the wall. Then Wendy walked in, documents in hand, dim and distorted almost lost in the blurry haze. Reaching out towards the thin shimmer of existence, his hand was immediately repelled, jolting back as if hit by a bolt of electricity. There was no lingering pain, just a mild tingle.

Frightened, he instinctively began racing towards the other end as fast as he could, but his legs soon betrayed him. He halted regaining his breath and continued, walking at a slow pace until he reached the far end. There he could see his house, his wife standing at the kitchen table preparing sandwiches and drinking her usual fix of coffee, even the rays of sunlight penetrating through the half-pulled blinds. Again it was blurry, milky, seemingly a step away, but in reality, further than conceivably possible. A wave of desperation and fear overwhelmed him. "Tina...!" he cried, his voice echoing and booming, but it was futile. He could now see his wife wandering away from the shimmer, disappearing into the vague depths of the other world.

Then suddenly, above his head, as if space, the universe itself, had opened up before him, there was darkness. This darkness extended down the length of the tunnel as far as the eye could see. He stood in terrified immobility. In a flash the solar system appeared before him... Neptune, Saturn, Jupiter, indeed all the planets revolving around the sun, like an atomic structure. The images changed. Now he could see the other worlds... galaxies, Andromeda, a spectrum of colours and varying patterns, hostile moisture-stripped planets, dull rotating spheres naked and barren, toxic atmospheres, dark cold crumpled rock layer after layer.

The expanding universe was now displayed in its totality. How and why he didn't know, but somehow in this dimension the images continued to roll but there were no signs of alien life. '*Where are they?*' he wondered, his theory beginning to collapse within him. Perhaps something else was responsible for creating man, life on Earth, something far greater than he could imagine, something beyond time and space and far more superior to imaginary aliens. The words of Astrophysicist Henry

Wicks had proven to be lies. His book was nothing but fabrication. Eric's distorted philosophy now faded into nothingness as other galaxies flashed before him, comets speeding through the universe, some consumed and swallowed by unknown forbidden planets. Still he looked on in fascination but no signs of alien life anywhere.

Suddenly, he was drawn towards the shimmering scene of his existence by an invisible energy field. In a flash and with a faint pop, as if the imaginary bubble of his dwelling had burst, he found himself inside his study at home, beside the T-propeller.

Sweating profusely, he looked up, gripping at reality, his reality as he knew it. Then to his overwhelming relief, he heard his wife's voice. He was now certain he had escaped the clutches of the other dimension.

"Darling, you took your time."

He rubbed his eyes, pale and exhausted, stripped of his dignity.

"Are you okay?"

"Yes, I'm fine," he mumbled, in a daze.

"By the way, Brett Ellman just called. He needed to speak to you urgently. Your invention may get on the market sooner than expected."

"Really," he said, collapsing into his gold leather chair, his lip curled. He motioned for the chair-manipulator to bring him a shot of brandy. He was in desperate need.

"I can't wait. Soon the entire planet will benefit from your marvellous invention. Hundreds of years from now you'll be remembered as one of the world's greatest pioneers. Eric love, they don't know what's in store for them."

He turned, gazed at it nervously, eyes round and wide.

"Yes indeed! They certainly don't...!".

The Appointment

"Hear me out," Earth Leader Vic Matuzak croaked, pointing, his old face alight with strict command. "As the appointed Ambassador of this planet, the responsibility lies solely with you." He raised his brow, his eyes peering intently, almost predatory.

"I hope I've made myself perfectly clear. Either they comply or else!"

"Yes Sir."

"Remember, no sting of conscience, no sentiment."

Ludovic stood, saluted, and turned almost rhythmically in military fashion, walking towards the door.

At the government headquarters Ludovic Martel sat at his oak desk, document in hand, his ashtray filled with cigarette-butts, the office redolent with their lingering stench. A lot was on his mind. In the walls hidden machinery whirred, discharging periodic wafts of ice-cold air into the room. Suddenly, the intercom buzzed into life.

"Sir, Jake De Quent is here."

"Okay Roger, escort him up," he grumbled with an elaborated casualness, continuing about his day.

A few minutes later Jake walked in, composed as always.

"Hi Ludovic. How was the meeting?"

"Okay, I guess. Just the same message! We're scheduled to leave tomorrow."

"Yes, I was told."

"What about you Jake, how's the research going?"

Sitting down he replied, "Good, real good. I've been working furiously at the Cosmic Centre looking over this planet Orious. Still find it hard to believe that it took us so long to discover it. We had all the systems mapped out, every planet."

"Well, it is located in another region of our galaxy. Who knows what else potentially lies out there." Ludovic cut off, gazing at him with glazed eyes.

"I guess so. Anyway, it's sixty thousand light years away. Hopefully we won't run into any meteor swarms before we reach the wormhole."

Jake pulled a document from his jacket, unrolling it.

"Here," he chimed eagerly, lips pressed together. "All the essential information with regards to Orious… It's all there, climate, temperature, its fixed periodic seasons, soil type, mineral deposits, air density, fauna and flora. Very similar to here. Almost uncanny. An oxygen nitrogen mix atmosphere."

Ludovic stretched it out across the desk, scanning, using a finger for guidance, his lips moving silently.

"It's the only one Ludovic… the only known planet in this entire galaxy which stands on its own away from our rule."

Ludovic watched Jake's eyes grow wide with anticipation as he contemplated his own words.

"Yet even after two long meetings with their representatives here on Earth, they still remain adamant, stubborn. They simply refuse to be a part of the galactic circle."

"For the moment," Ludovic replied sharply. "You see Jake our visit there will change things."

"I doubt it. They are locked into their own system... an ancient religious system of some type, I believe. Besides they've known about us for years. According to their leader, Earth has been a planet they have taken great interest in, analysing it from their com-modules, checking us out, studying it rigorously. In all that time they have never once wanted to contact us or any of our colonies. That, in itself, tells the story."

"You'll be surprised how things can change with the right application Jake."

"Ludovic, between you and me I'm not too sure about this one. They will never conform to the galactic culture or law. It's as if they purposely want to maintain a religious archaic-like existence, even though it appears to keep up with our technocratic levels... at least from what we know. They certainly appear to have made similar progressive advancements on their own... who knows? Perhaps they have other things that we don't know of, greater things, greater inventions."

"Regardless Jake, the purpose of this trip is to send them a message, a final ultimatum. Either they sign..."

His face became hard and cynical. He clenched his fist. His eyes held no emotion.

"Or?"

"Or we blow them out of existence..."

The immense ship entered the planet's atmosphere, swooping towards a giant spaceport in a glowing blur of energy. Dials and meters swung into activity, registering, humming. Descent lights flickered. Across the gleaming control board, the co-pilot spun a dial releasing a series of signals, which the base monitor below recorded.

"I've received clearance," the co confirmed to the head-pilot.

Rapidly, with precision, they descended, the landscape of the planet now coming into view. As the ship landed, a tide of energy shook the ground. Acceleration dials fell to zero. At last they had arrived after a four-day journey. Technicians suddenly appeared, rushing out from small surveillance-huts, busy little dots dressed in grey, circling around the ship, inspecting for metal fatigue and stress fractures. Ship monitoring surface-vehicles lurched from side to side, a bustle of efficient motion.

Both Ludovic and Jake walked down the ramp with eager strides, gazing around arrogantly. A surge of adrenaline raced through them both. Overhead, the sky was dull and cloudy, the air humid and hot. Barren fields surrounded the spaceport, burned clean of any vegetation, beyond it an undulating expanse of green, a verdant countryside which stretched towards a metropolis, a tiny flickering dot in the distance.

"Do you realise Jake? We are finally here. We've made history but it's imperative we remain focused on the task."

A long blue vehicle suddenly pulled up, slowing to a halt. An elegantly dressed man stepped out from the driver's seat and calmly walked over, his heels clattering against the ground. He was tall and slim, his blue eyes warm.

"Clarence Marvin, Cultural Attaché and for today your driver as well..." He half bowed and smiled his face aglow with sincerity.

"Ludovic Martel, Terra Ambassador." He shook his hand awkwardly with mixed emotions, folder under his arm. "This is Professor Jake De Quent, Chief Scientist for the government."

"Nice to meet you both... Please let's be on our way. Our leader is anticipating your arrival. We have exactly one hour before the meeting at the palace. You'll both find the back seats very comfortable."

They were on a hot steaming highway, blending in with the endless tide of surface-vehicles. Ludovic sat in silence gazing through the window at the green countryside. In the distance a winged creature hovered, skimming the surface of the planet. The clouds had now subsided. The sun shone and the sky sparkled into being, restoring light and colour to the land, trees and hills and endless valleys. Above, jets hummed, circling the sky, commuters returning from work, slender metallic crafts of countless kinds.

"You've got some neat looking jets here, Mr Marvin."

"Oh yes Mr Martel, indeed we do. They are the latest and very special... free from the force of gravity."

"What...! You mean to say you have anti-gravity technology?"

"Yes, newly discovered, an amazing technological invention. When our representatives journeyed to Earth for those two recent meetings, they used an anti-gravity ship."

Ludovic and Jake gazed at each other in total astonishment.

"Did you hear that, Jake?"Ludovic whispered in his companion's ear. "Incredible! You were right. They do have other things... things that we can benefit from once we take over."

Seconds of silence passed...

"By the way, gentlemen, just for your information, we are about to enter the robot quarters of the city."

"Robot quarters...? What kind of government would implement such a law, segregating robots from its creators?" Ludovic muttered to himself nudging Jake, who seemed equally perturbed.

"Mr Marvin, have you always had this city set up this way? Your kind living in one part of the city, robots in the other...?"

"Yes of course, Mr Martel. As liberal as we are, we've always understood that man and machine must live separately. Machines are there for the sole purpose of serving man... nothing more. Of course they are treated with scientific respect, but each to their own. Most take on economic and industrial functions."

Jake interjected, "You see, down on Earth and throughout the galaxy, robots live with humans functioning in unanimity."

"I can believe it, but not here..."

The surface-vehicle took a sharp turn, 'Exit Wallisberg.' Passing through a long winding tunnel they entered a huge city, a cacophony of endless sounds. Chaos filled the air. Robots were scattered everywhere, bright hulls of metal standing in groups, conversing, streaming in and out of buildings, speeding on glider bikes, each and everyone engaged in some kind of activity. Further on, a conglomeration of towering structures soared into the atmosphere, endless spires rising like needles, diffusing a golden glow emanating from the specialised alloys.

"Quite an advanced looking city Mr Marvin," Ludovic said, absorbing the surroundings.

"Indeed, Mr Martel, indeed. Everything on Orious is built with high precision and beauty. It's uniform, a standard we maintain throughout the planet unremittingly."

After some time they reached the human quarters, driving down a long road, past the main intersection, colourful flowers and well pruned tress on either side. On a hill, a group of workers sprinkled water onto the soil, labouring away energetically. Beside them, an unusual looking animal munched on the grass, its great eyes half shut with fatigue. An elaborate white palace now came into view, compelling in its grandeur and innovative style.

"We're here Jake," Ludovic whispered from the corner of his mouth. The decisive moment had come.

Inside the confines of the palace, they were escorted into a large office, meticulously arranged. From the white ceiling, an elegant chandelier hung. Beams of sunlight filtered through the windows, sparkling across the marble floor, the room reflected in its polished surface. The windows were wide, with heavy brass handles; somewhat odd for a world which had evidently kept up with the technocratic levels of the cosmos, and indeed, excelled in so many areas. Ludovic shook his head in disbelief at his fleeting impression of the room.

"Look Jake," he muttered quietly. "They have anti-gravity technology at their disposal, yet they still open windows by hand."

"Please gentlemen, take a seat," the Attaché said. "Our leader will be with you in a moment."

Turning, he left, his footsteps fading into silence. They were now completely alone. Ludovic sat down and unzipped his folder, taking out the one document of vital importance.

"We'll get this over with quickly, sharp and concise."

Jake winked, acknowledging mutely. A discreet smile passed across his face. Suddenly the doors opened. The leader of Orious walked in, imperially, dressed in a long grey cloak which slithered across the floor behind him, almost a mythological character. He was bald and clean shaven. His ancient eyes shone like two black pearls, ablaze with energy, an energy that appeared to consume the actual organ of sight itself. It went beyond the individual, beyond anything carnal.

His profound inner wisdom was displayed structurally across his face, reflected in his features. A strange thrill shot through them both, a deep sense of awe. Ludovic uncomfortably wondered why that should be.

"Welcome... I'm Miryandis, Leader of Orious."

The quality of his voice held a great resonance, his words spaced apart, yet powerful. It demanded attention.

Swallowing hard, Ludovic introduced himself.

"Ludovic Martel, Earth Ambassador."

"Jake De Quent, Chief Scientist..."

"So gentlemen what brings you here with such urgency? I believe our two representatives have already established our standing with regards to the future of this planet."

Ludovic shuffled, adjusting himself, his posture and facial expression unveiling the seriousness of his business.

"Mr Miryandis, I come here with strict orders. Please, if you will?"

He pushed forward the legal document. A period of silence followed as Miryandis read rapidly, his expression unreadable throughout. The tension in the room was almost tangible. It mounted as the silence grew. Then...

"So this is what it's come to?" He shook his head slowly.

"Afraid so," Ludovic replied. He knew the implications of this document were vast for the man facing him and for this world. He needed to add emphasis.

"Sir, you must understand one thing, we control the systems throughout. We are the central source, implementing the laws and rules, cultural trends and so forth. Each solar system, each planet throughout the galaxy comes under one galactic hat, one universal rule, one way of living, Earth's way!"

Miryandis gazed at them silently before replying.

"It appears to me that you are devoid of certain facts. This planet, dear Sirs, is a very special planet, a jewel in space. As we have already stated, there is no way we will allow you to forcefully change our way of life. We have lived in peace and harmony for years... that won't alter."

"Perhaps *you* don't understand," Jake now said harshly. "We have been authorised to blow you out of existence if you refuse to sign. It's there in black and white."

"So be it."

Ludovic intervened. "Are you honestly refusing to acknowledge us as the power here? For the sake of one simple signature you would rather cease to exist, killing billions of others in the process."

"Indeed, maybe so," Miryandis muttered softly. "But signing that document would bring this planet to an end regardless...only then it would be a slow gradual death."

"What do you mean?" Ludovic asked forehead creased.

"Here on Orious we have our own laws which we adhere to rigorously. This has been the platform for our success. We, alone, have developed our own technology, created our own industries, our own methods, our own realities. For us to be ruled by you and come under the 'galactic hat' as you call it, is totally unacceptable. The changes would be radically negative."

"But why? Our methods are coherent, well thought out, full of integrated valid factors... controlled and maintained from a central source on Earth. And as for your position... it wouldn't be affected in the slightest. You would still govern the planet, under our guidance... under our law."

"Mr Martel, there is no way."

He rested his bare elbows upon the desk, pressing his hands together.

"Your laws are diametrically opposed to ours. They're based around control, an iron hand, brute force and fear. Here we place emphasis on love."

"Brute force and fear, Mr Miryandis, is the best way to control the masses. We have colonized the systems throughout the galaxy by adapting this methodology."

Rubbing his forehead, Miryandis said, "You and the people of Earth have killed many throughout the galaxy. In startling contrast, our methods here are founded on love. It's the only way. It conquers death and the fear of it. We will never accept the false ideologies that you impose... never!"

"Ideologies," Jake blasted. "Such as...?"

"Atheism!"

The word ricocheted around the room. Ludovic, despite his many years of experience, only now recognised Miryandis' contained rage.

"The galactic law is dominated by an atheistic philosophy, is it not? There is no way we could ever embrace it. Death is better."

"What!" Jake snapped. "How can you question fact? We are the product of evolution, nothing but animals, evolved monkeys. There is no Creator."

Ludovic interjected.

"Just what is your problem with that?"

"Gentlemen, yes, we agree evolution took place but, in our view theistically speaking. In other words God is the mechanism behind evolution... theistic evolution. Atheistic evolution makes no sense! God, via the laws of evolution, created the universe. He was the force behind this highly complex process. Things just don't self-evolve accidentally. It required a technician to orchestrate it."His voice was now filled with passion... awe!

"Man's existence is down to a Creator of supreme power, as are all the other complex life forms, such as animals, fish, and insects. But man is a very special creature, distinctly separate from any living thing. We humans, no matter where we are located in the universe, are nothing short of a miracle. From the point of conception to birth, from a child to adulthood, in that life cycle there are clear miraculous progressive stages of change, growth, biological and chemical modifications, if you like, which are manifested externally, structurally. Is that all down to chance? It is the human brain gentlemen, a powerful electrochemical organ that sets us apart from any animal, any creature... the cerebral cortex."

They watched him apprehensively, shocked by his profound discourse.

"In spite of all our steadily accumulated knowledge, the mechanisms of the brain still remain a profound mystery. How could such an amazing organ develop on its own? Surely you must acknowledge the existence of a superior intellect. If I told you the ship that brought you here just suddenly appeared from nowhere, would you believe it? It required a designer, a builder, did it not? How much greater is the human brain? Right now an incredible interchange of chemical and electrical activity is taking place in our heads, breath-taking neurological activity."

Ludovic sat in agitated silence. Something deep within him had ignited; something he himself couldn't explain. The words rumbled through him poetically, causing him to reflect with reverence and growing enlightenment. He suppressed his reaction, masking it well. Miryandis continued.

"You see, the consequences of your atheistic philosophy stretch further than you could ever imagine. Think about the psychological impact that atheism has had on you. Think about the implications that come with atheism. To accept that you are just the product of a mistake will surely affect the way you view yourself and others around you in a very negative way. It will affect your view of morality; it will affect your decisions, your mind-set as a whole. Everything ultimately becomes meaningless. Morality and God go hand in hand. Morality has to be built around our love for God. Without God, ethics and morality become subjective. This is the essence of sin, that we become dictator of what is right and wrong. Without God being at the centre of our lives, the very foundation of our being, man is simply eternally lost... Now, in your law book it states that an explosion set life into motion, thus creating everything that we see. Gentlemen, the Big Bang did take place, but it was God who was behind this complex explosion. He was the technician behind the Big Bang."

"This is preposterous," Jake rumbled, his jaw jutting out in anger."

"Please allow me to finish and fully convey my message."

Miryandis paused momentarily.

"Ask yourselves, what is the purpose of human life? It's such a short journey, and at times a painful one. We are very special, created for a purpose... a reason."

"Which is?" queried Ludovic.

"Relationship... Everything around us is about relationship. We see it with insects, animals, and of course humans. There is a special interrelationship throughout the cosmos and beyond. Without relationship we are nothing. We need it to be certain of ourselves, our existence and our place in the universe."

Jake rose from his chair, his face a mask of rage, eyes cold with hostility. He interjected.

"You are living in a world of your own Miryandis."

"Yes, indeed and like that it shall remain."

"Mr Miryandis," Jake blasted icily sitting back down. "We haven't journeyed here for a theological debate. This is political. Are you saying that the only reason you refuse to sign is because our laws are based around an atheistic philosophy, and that theism is banned from our law?"

"Yes indeed. Your atheistic philosophy is a weapon of destruction! It makes up the very foundation of your law. Theism is the key to everything. The key to life... Man needs God. Without God man is void and empty, without a purpose, an objective. Without God, we lose our way, our meaning our identity. We become dictator of what is right and wrong with a distorted, subjective view. We lose sight of our existence, our relationship with others, with devastating consequences. Without God we are spiritually dead. To sign that document would mean spiritual death. Your faith gentlemen, is a weapon of ultimate destruction."

"Faith? We have no faith Mr Miryandis," snapped Jake.

"Professor Jake De Quent, to believe that this universe appeared out of nothing and ultimately self-evolved requires more faith than believing in a creator."

"Nonsense!"

"What do you mean?" Ludovic inquired curiously.

"Well, let's use a basic mathematical formula to illustrate my point. Logical application is the key. Indulge me. From a mathematical standpoint atheism is basically saying this... that zero multiplied by zero equals everything! This is totally illogical, irrational, and completely absurd. The only equation that works is this... God via his almighty power brought all life into existence."

Ludovic's eyes grew wide with awe. But Jake's face hardened as Miryandis continued.

"When you apply logic, you realise that atheism requires far more faith than you could ever imagine, far more than theism."

"But who created this God?" asked Ludovic.

"This is a non-question. This is known as circular reasoning, the fundamental fallacy in logic. By definition, God is eternal, thus you cannot ask such a question. Furthermore, God is and always will be. He is eternal. He is not bound by time. He is outside the sphere of time and space. He dwells in eternity, the Alpha and Omega. He can see the past, present and future in an instant. We who are locked in time cannot comprehend God's eternal being... it is impossible. The eternality of God transcends science and human understanding. God simply is."

A deafening silence fell.

"Now, let me enlighten you both further. The universe is a marvel of mathematical order. Immense and complex, filled with billions of galactic clusters. The human brain hasn't even begun to comprehend its mysteries. Look at your solar system, your planet, Earth... It's one of the greatest cosmological scientific puzzles, confounding our efforts to understand it. It's where all life began. We are its descendants; a ball of clay filled with majestic colourful panoramas, it thrives with life and motion, sustained by very complex systems that provide, air, light, water and food in exquisite balance. As it orbits the sun once a year the Earth travels at an average speed of 30kilometres per second, 67,000 miles per hour. Even its tilt allows for the seasonal changes. Indeed life throughout the cosmos is characterized by this mind-blowing arrangement, starting at an atomic level."

Miryandis stood up his eyes ablaze with energy, his face wise with profundity. He continued...

"My friends, the universe demands a creator of supreme power and intelligence. Everything around us is a living miracle, from a microscopic organism to a human being."

"Mr Miryandis, you have a marvellously convoluted mind, but you are missing the whole point of this meeting. Let's not deviate from the point any further."

"On the contrary, my dear Jake... Listen carefully. Allow me to enlighten you further. We are nothing but a cluster of atoms. Atoms are like miniature solar systems forming covalent bonds due to a deficient number of orbiting electrons, which in turn form molecules, DNA... RNA strands... proteins, the building blocks to life. In short, the atom that lacks an electron, the unstable atom, looks to merge with another atom to make up for its missing electron. This is covalent bonding. This whole process only occurs due to a deficient number of orbiting electrons. As a result life begins. Atoms inter-combine and form very complex molecules, proteins, DNA, and so forth. Then the whole evolutionary process begins. Thus, life starts as a result of an imperfection at an atomic level. Now the cell is like a miniature world of its own, a living factory alive with highly complex activity far more complex than anything known to man. To fully understand what takes place in the nucleus of a cell is mind blowing."

Jake banged his fist against the desk, his face full of stubborn dignity.

"That's enough. It ends here. Sign or else!"

"Enough?" Miryandis replied piercingly, jabbing his finger towards him. Sudden authority stiffened his voice.

"Professor Jake De Quent sometimes the truth cuts so deep that only anger can rise up in an attempt to heal such a wound but there is no repair, only acceptance... acceptance and the realisation that we are imperfect beings in desperate need of change. The journey of life is like a grain of sand drifting through the ocean of time, swinging between a pendulum of life and death with an inevitable end. Our lives here will dictate our final fate, our final destination. It lies in our hands..."

Ludovic looked at Jake trying to convey his inner conflicting emotions. Jake in turn remained focused, fuelled by loyalty and blind adherence to the law.

"It's your choice Miryandis. You have decided your own fate... with it, that of a planet."

"No Jake De Quent, you are trapped, trapped in a state of cognitive dissonance and circular reasoning, the fundamental fallacy in logic... imprisoned by foolishness and delusions of grandeur, a warped mind. Your view of life is diametrically opposed to the truth. In order to attain the truth, you need to break free from the sphere of your own domain."

Seconds of silence passed.

"I leave you with this. You may take our lives, you may destroy a planet, but you will never kill the truth, never."

Back in the ship, far out, afloat in space, Ludovic stood gazing at the slowly fading planet, his eyes deep troubled and profound. The laser vaporizer had been set, its target Orious. Sitting beside the activator in his green luminous uniform was the military co-pilot, awaiting the vital command.

"Sir, all set. We are just about at the right distance for activation." He looked through the target monitor, mapping out the precise location of impact.

Ludovic was still, ripples of sweat forming across his brow. The final words of Miryandis swept within him, echoing... tearing him apart. It had left all kinds of existential questions resonating in his mind. He was caught in a spiral of confused emotion.

"Well," Jake grated impatiently from behind, seated in his revolving chair, tilting back, legs crossed. Ludovic glanced back at him.

"Give the command. Soon Orious will be non-existent, nothing but a blazing mass of fire and ash... a few drifting rocks afloat in space."

He smirked, eyes cold as he pictured the destruction. The co-pilot sat rigidly, ready, finger on the activator.

"Jake I... I can't."

He let it out in an unsteady rush of relief, running a shaky hand through his hair. Jake leapt to his feet.

"What! Am I talking with Ludovic Martel?"

"You heard me... I can't."

"Have you lost your mind? What the heck has gotten into you?"

"There are billions of people down there, children, families!" He pointed with anguished concern. "Who am I to take life? Who are we to decide the fate of a planet?"

"You, as the Ambassador, were given strict orders. You have two choices... either you comply, or you face serious consequences. This won't be taken lightly. How could you allow that half crazed man to twist your mind?"

"Twist? No Jake, he unlocked something within me, far more profound than anything the material world can offer. His words were too eloquent, his logic wise and precise. An untamed wisdom that supersedes anything I've encountered; a master of dialectics. Man doesn't live forever. What lies beyond death? This is something that we need to think about. We can't dismiss it! To embrace atheism as the ultimate truth is our biggest downfall. Our time here is almost non-existent, a mere blink in the face of eternity. We get so caught up in the spiral of life that we seldom sit back and realise we are mortal beings with an end. The fear of death has always been our greatest enemy, the very knowledge of our own mortality. With certainty all life will cease and then?"

"And then what?"

"Who knows Jake, who knows? It's something we need to think about."

Ludovic began walking towards the metallic passageway, his steps dragging as though depleted of energy. Suddenly he halted, turning, his hand pressed against the steel of the wall, his knuckles white. Both Jake and the co-pilot were motionless, mouths gaping in disbelief...

"I guess I'll have a lot of explaining to do when we get back, ugh?"

He moved on, leaving nothing but silence in his trail except for the roar of the ship, as it continued its journey, piercing through the trackless void of eternity.

The Hidden Cave

Steering the speedboat to its maximum capacity, away from the fading coastline of San Francisco, with trained, narrowed eyes, Pete Ellis turned and said, "Just a couple of more kilometres and we'll stop."

Cliff Fontaine smiled in acknowledgment. Sitting rigidly in his wetsuit, he regulated his oxygen tank. A routine dive awaited him, one born out of adventure rather than necessity, the ocean luring him, a mysterious world with an ecosystem of its own.

Across the warm waters of the Pacific, darkness was now descending. Standing in his flippers, Cliff moved over towards Pete with controlled effort. There was no expression on his face, a stone-like detachment as he psyched himself up for the task at hand.

Easing the throttle, they came to a gradual halt, the engine ticking over quietly. The boat, now immobile, began to roll and bounce gently. Engulfing them in all directions were miles of ocean water, dark and eerie. Above, the moon appeared large and luminous, casting its reflection over the face of the sea. A red warning light suddenly flashed, signalling low fuel.

"Pete, I hope we have enough to get back."

"Don't worry, it's an electrical malfunction... we've got plenty." He switched off the engine.

Cliff's initial concern was nullified. As an eminent Marine Biologist and skilled scuba-diver, everything had to be done methodically. It was part of his character and of course fundamental to the line of work he was in. He glanced up and Pete knew he was judging the positioning of the stars, the sidereal cycle, the tides, and his inner sense of chronology to guess the hour. It was a sort of ritual for Cliff. Then he consulted his wristwatch for confirmation. Pete checked his own. The glowing dials showed 21:00 hours.

"Okay, I'm ready," Cliff said brightly, making his final checks then tightening the strap of his buoyancy compensator around his waist. Moving to the edge of the boat, one step at a time maintaining equilibrium, he sat facing Pete.

"Give me fifty minutes... if I'm not up by then, you know what to do."

Pete laughed. "Hey, come on, I'm sure the sharks have gotten used to you by now."

Before lowering his mask, Cliff winked and smiled, a smile full of confidence that Pete envied. The ocean, the darkness, and the feverish fears that came with his passion, never hindered him nor blocked that surging rush of excitement and hunger within. Focused and alert, he fixed the mask across his face, securing the demand valve around his gums. Then raising a thumb he fell backwards into the sea with a splash. All that was left on the surface was a pool of foam and a deafening silence.

Descending into what looked like a cloudy abyss, Cliff stretched out his left arm activating the torch with the click of a switch. Light refraction was a minor impediment, but he remained focused, solely dependent on the hazy beam of light which guided him further and further into the unknown. With a sharp twist of his body and a swift wiggle of his feet, he suddenly plunged down vertically, gaining depth rapidly. The darkness grew, with it his adrenal fix and that inner hunger to explore the unknown. Reaching the sandy ocean bed of the Pacific, he halted and began moving the torch in a sideways motion. With poor visibility, all he could distinguish was a vast array of exotic looking corals. He felt at peace, away from the roar and commotion of the world.

Then unexpectedly, from out of nowhere, as if someone had turned on a switch, a light began emanating from what looked like a cave. Intrigued by what he saw, he began manoeuvring towards the entrance, almost as if magnetically attracted. This brilliant, seemingly endless light had an extraordinary glow about it, alien-like. As he drew closer, he became totally absorbed in it. There was a sense of detachment, creating a dream-like effect beyond reality.

Slowly he entered and was at once alerted to the fact that the light appeared to emanate from nowhere. Turning and twisting, he couldn't comprehend where it was coming from. His discernment had temporarily abandoned him. He was a man of science. Everything had to be based on logic but not this time. This baffling phenomenon began to lure him in further, rather than repel him. A school of colourful fish suddenly shot past darting away into the distance, shattering his attention. As he breathed in his canned oxygen, he raised his wrist to the face of his mask to consult his watch. To his surprise it was malfunctioning, the dials spinning anticlockwise at great speed, nearly invisible to the eye. Before he even had a chance to be concerned by this he felt faint, almost losing consciousness. He fought it, shaking his head vigorously; the blur and dizziness now beginning to fade. Gradually he regained composure and a steady thought pattern. Guided by survival instincts, he darted out of the luminous cave, and began a prompt, controlled ascent.

The unexpected urge to escape the clutches of the ocean was mounting by the second; his ascent seemed to take an eternity. As he surfaced, there was a raging storm, waves tossing to and fro, rumbles of thunder echoing, lightening illuminating the sky dazzling white. Cold hard rain pelted down, the heavens dark and miserable, a thick grey cloud belt twisting and moving, concealing the night spheres. Within seconds he saw the boat, and the dim figure of Pete waving him over. The wind picked up speed, howling and swishing around without respite.

"Pete," he cried, the demand valve stifling his voice, the muffled tones vibrating through his facial bones and mask.

In a quick burst, Cliff swam his way over battling through the oncoming ice-cold waves. It was testing, but he fought through until he reached the side of the boat. Pete knelt, lowering his hand in support.

"Steady," he gasped, the cords in his neck rippling with tension and strain.

Grasping Pete's outstretched hand, Cliff climbed aboard, sliding the mask from his face. Pulling the demand valve from his mouth, he coughed. His normal breathing pattern was rapidly restored.

"Are you okay Cliff? The weather just took a turn. It's getting pretty bad. We'll have to head back immediately."

"Pete, wait, listen... I had the most bizarre experience down below."

Pete was silent... curious.

"There was a light.... a bright light coming from a cave. It just happened all of a sudden."

"Are you serious? Did you investigate?"

"Yeah, but..."

"But what?"

The storm began to worsen, rocking the boat violently, causing loose equipment to slide around on deck, some plunging overboard.

"I think we'd better make headway. You can tell me later."

"Guess so," Cliff replied, his voice dull and strained, his face filled with bewilderment.

With the roar of the engine, they commenced their journey back to shore, bouncing and dipping over the face of the angered sea.

"Cliff honey wake up, it's almost twelve."

Opening his dark, fatigued eyes, sleep began to dissolve, the cream-coloured ceiling and the world around him coming into focus. In the background he could hear the radio, the usual morning dose of Country and Western resonating dimly in his ears. He threw his hand in its direction lowering the volume into silence.

"Cliff," his wife said again, now capturing his attention. "Are you ever going to give me a moment of your time? You and the ocean... Never a moment for us..."

His wife stood there peering over at him closely, her hand resting at her hip awaiting a reply. He stretched out his hand tugging her towards him.

"Sandy babe," He smiled playfully, now fully alert to his surroundings. "This compulsion and obsession of mine has given us a lavish lifestyle, one which you seem to enjoy."

He cupped her chin in the palm of his hand, gazing into her eyes. They kissed, an intimate kiss, warm and tender. At that moment, the door swung open, halting halfway. Billy rushed in, red cheeked, chocolate smudged across his lips and striped vest.

"Daddy," he cried in his squeaky voice, jumping across the bed into his father's reassuring arms.

"Hey, little man. No school today?"

"Cliff, it's a holiday," his wife replied fixing her heavy mass of golden hair in the mirror."

The phone rang, shattering the warm family atmosphere. Sandy lifted the receiver.

"Honey, it's Pete."

She walked over handing him the phone, then left the room with Billy following mischievously behind.

"Hey Cliff, how's it going?"

"Okay I guess." He yawned, eyes shut. "Just here with the family, but still none the wiser as to last night's strange underwater encounter. That light, that cave and that's not all."

He frowned as he recaptured the moment.

"Oh yeah that's right," Pete replied brightly, "I mentioned it to Brad this morning."

"Brad? Brad who?"

"Brad Stevens. Who else?"

Cliff was puzzled.

"Pete, I don't know a Brad Stevens."

"What! Are you joking? You've known him for more than ten years."

A moment of hesitation.

"Cliff, are you certain you're okay?"

Cliff clung tighter to the phone, mute and immobile, broken dream-like thoughts and theories racing through his mind.

"In answer to your question it all depends on whether you're being serious... Pete," his voice grew in pitch tinged with an element of annoyance, "I don't know any Brad."

"Wait, are you honestly saying you have no knowledge or recollection of him?" Cliff could here Pete's growing concern in his voice.

"Yes, that's precisely what I'm saying."

"Look buddy, I don't know what happened to you last night, but it appears you've suffered some kind of memory loss. The implications of what you encountered may be vast. I think we need to talk. I'll come by right away."

As the call ended, Cliff was lost in a haze of worry and confusion. Placing the phone on the bed, he made his way to the door, pausing at the spiral staircase. After a few seconds of contemplation, he headed to the kitchen where Sandy stood washing a stack of dirty dishes. She seemed to sense something was wrong.

"Babe, you okay?"

"Not sure..."

He scratched his head nervously, seating himself at the breakfast table, trying to regain his composure, the bright kitchen lights clearly demarking his thought drenched features.

"I don't understand," she replied, "Not sure about what?"

"Tell me, do we know a Brad Stevens? Or perhaps I should rephrase it.... do I know a Brad Stevens?"

His mystified eyes grew wide as he looked at her, almost willing her to say no. Sandy walked over and sat beside him, puzzled, taken aback by the question.

"Cliff honey, are you serious?"

"Evidently so..."

An interval of silence.

"Babe... we've known Brad and Sally-Anne Stevens for over ten years now. Why are you asking me such a stupid question?"

His face lit with panic, his jaw rigid, teeth locked.

"Sandy, it's because I have never met this person, nor do I have any recollection of him... or, in fact, them..."

"Cliff stop clowning, you're worrying me."

At that moment the doorbell rang, breaking the tense atmosphere.

"I'll get that," Sandy said walking away anxiously.

Minutes later, Pete stepped into the kitchen, Sandy following behind.

"Hi Cliff, how are you feeling?"

"Pete, listen to me, I know what you are thinking, but please believe me, I'm not suffering from a neurological disorder nor am I suffering from memory loss."

Pete walked over and sat facing him, Sandy motionless in the corner, hugging herself in anxiety.

"What Cliff... What are you suggesting then?" He crossed his legs leaning back eyeing him analytically.

"I don't know myself."

"Cliff this is bizarre, totally bizarre. Brad has been your dear friend for the last ten years. Do you honestly have no recollection of him at all?"

Cliff didn't answer. He began to stare at the surroundings with a cold hard expression on his face. Oddly everything around him seemed different, tiny details like the positioning of the breakfast table, the ambience, the flowery scent in the air. He was engulfed by a number of peculiarities; the fear was minor in comparison to his awareness of the baffling predicament he was in.

"What is it, Cliff?" Pete asked abruptly, jerking him out of his daze. Sandy approached, her face pallid... anxious.

"There, that picture... that picture above the sink. I don't recall that being there."

"Sweetheart, it's been there ever since we moved in five years ago."

She eyed Pete with alarm. He acknowledged her bewilderment and returned the same mystified stare.

"Cliff, are you saying you don't recall that picture?"

"No Pete, I remember the picture alright, but I don't recall it being located there. In fact we had it hanging upstairs, in the bedroom."

He pointed to affirm that was indeed the case, although deep down, he was beginning to question his sanity.

"Look, I think you should get some rest. Tomorrow morning I'll have an appointment booked."

Before he could finish, Cliff interrupted. "With whom Pete...? A psychiatrist...?" He paused. "It's as if..."

"Go on," Sandy urged with wide apprehensive eyes, holding onto his shoulder.

"It's as if there's a distinct barrier between me and this... this reality... this world. Damn!" he yelled leaping to his feet, his face filled with ripples of tension.

Walking over to the sink he halted, frozen to the spot and stood gazing through the window towards the still, quiet sidewalk. Then, with a submissive acceptance, he held his hand to his forehead.

"This is futile. Sandy, call Doctor White, see if you can fix me an urgent appointment."

Without replying, she ran into the corridor and sprang towards the phone.

At the Doctor's Surgery, Cliff was called over by the receptionist. It was his turn to see Dr White. As he stood there, Sandy tugged his jacket.

"Shall I come in with you?"

"No, it's ok, don't worry."

He forced a broken washed-out smile, a bold attempt to allay Sandy's growing fears. As transparent as it was, it gave her a flicker of hope, something to hold onto.

Slowly, he made his way over, halting by the reception desk, where a neat looking brunette directed him through. Inside the Doctor's office, Cliff slumped into a brown leather chair. The Doctor adjusted his tie and began.

"So Professor Fontaine, how can I help?"

There was no immediate reply, just a long, extended exchange of calculated glances.

"Sorry Doc, I just don't know how to convey this to you without your instantly assuming that I'm suffering from some kind of neurological disorder."

"Let me be the judge of that."

"This morning, whilst in discussion with a dear friend and colleague he mentioned someone, a person... a person that I have never heard of, nor had any kind of interaction with for that matter. When I told him I had never known him, this left him stunned, bewildered."

"Why?" the Doctor inquired, keen interest in his voice.

"Why? It's because..." He began to fidget and clasp his hands tightly. "It's because he claims I've known him for over ten years, and that's not all. My wife Sandy confirms that this is indeed the case."

"Extraordinary... Tell me, have you had any other strange encounters? I mean anything equally bizarre as what you just told me?"

"No, not exactly, but there are other things. For example, in the kitchen, hanging over the sink is a picture...but that picture was never there, I know it for a fact."

"Where was it then?"

"Hanging in the bedroom. When I told my wife, she was adamant that it had been there ever since we moved in five years ago... but I tell you that's not the case."

"Sir, these are a strange series of delusions. I see from your medical records you have never suffered from any type of psychological problem. To assume that you are now is clearly not the case... you are so rational and coherent in your approach and explanation... your mind, lucid."

"So what's happening to me then?"

"Memory loss, temporary memory loss at this stage it's the most probable diagnosis."

He halted, absorbed in profound thought.

"Tell me, have you been under any stress lately or can you think of anything that may have triggered such a condition?"

For the first time since his strange underwater encounter, Cliff began to wonder whether there was some kind of connection. There simply had to be. '*What was* that *light?*' he thought pensively. '*Where did it come from?*'

He suddenly said, "Doc, last night I was out diving."

"Okay..."

"And then..." Cliff broke off and swallowed hard, as if searching for the correct words to use. "A strange light," his voice rose as he pictured it... "There was this strange light emanating from an underwater cave. It happened all so suddenly."

Intrigued, the Doctor sat up straight, putting his fingers to his lips.

"Please continue."

"As I entered the cave, the light source appeared to shine from out of nowhere."

"Were you alone the whole time?"

"Yes, yes I was."

"What occurred next?"

"My watch started malfunctioning, the dials spinning at great speed. Then I almost lost consciousness. I'm a vastly experienced diver. I have never encountered such a phenomenon. It's as if, as if it came from another world."

Struck by his own words, he suddenly paused. Images and metaphysical theories began flashing through his mind, accompanied by a foreboding sensation that became a fully blown revelation.

"Another world being the operative word," he said under his breath, barely moving his lips.

"What was that?"

"Thanks Doc, that'll be all."

Cliff leapt up, heading for the door ignoring the doctor's protests. Despair cut through him. His pulse altered... his stomach knotting.

"Professor Fontaine, please!"

He glanced back briefly to see the doctor standing behind his desk, biting his lip, pensive and puzzled. It was no use, he was gone. He shut the door, grabbed Sandy by the arm and hurried from the surgery.

On the way home, Cliff sat fixed to the passenger seat, gazing at the stars as if he found refuge in them, gripping onto something he could clearly identify and familiarize himself with. Across from him, in the silence, sat Sandy, her trim shape and pretty features faintly visible in the gloom. She looked anxious, preoccupied.

"Cliff, you shouldn't have left like that. You just stormed out of there like a crazed man."

"Sandy, please… don't make me repeat myself." He felt a twinge of guilt. He knew she was concerned but he did not have the capacity to deal with that right now.

Ahead, the beaming lights of a passing truck swept into the car. Its engine groaned and rumbled noisily. It passed them by, descending down the road, away into the distance.

As they arrived home, the outside house lights activated, filtering through the vine-entangled entrance and reflecting against the hood of the car. He flung the door open and stepped out into the zone of light, lifeless leaves crunching under the weight of his feet. A few drifted past him, tossed by the wind into the vast cloud of night. By the foyer, the weather-beaten rocking chair creaked. The night chill brought with it a wind which swished around, almost pulling him in the direction of the door. Entering the dimly lit hallway, Billy came rushing over in his green pyjamas, wild joy leaping through him.

"Mommy, Daddy."

"Hi Mrs Fontaine," the nanny said stepping out from the kitchen, her old, wrinkled face alive and chirpy. "He's just finished supper… time for homework."

"You heard Ms Watson Billy, off you go," ordered Sandy gently. Bending, she kissed him, and then with a pat and rub on the head, little blond Billy darted off, dashing up the stairs almost losing his footing.

"Thanks Ms Watson."

"Pleasure madam. Just give me a call whenever I'm needed."

In the library under a bright table lamp, Cliff sat reading a book entitled: Parallel Universe Theory: It said, 'Our universe is absolutely immense. Planet Earth is one of eight planets that revolve around our sun, which is a star, and there are billions or maybe even trillions of stars in the Milky Way galaxy. With existing technology, we can see well beyond our own galaxy into the observable universe, which has a diameter of 92 billion light-years and contains perhaps two trillion galaxies. Evidence indicates the universe is much, much bigger than we can actually observe and might be infinitely large. Parallel universe theory explores the possibility that the universe contains planets and galaxies similar to our own, or even that an infinite number of separate universes may form a grand multiverse. The concept of a multiverse arises from inflation theory, string theory and of course, quantum mechanics.

The universe, space and time, started with the Big Bang. However, there were some aspects of the Big Bang that could not be explained until inflation theory was introduced. Inflation theory explains what happened in the tiny fraction of a second before the Big Bang. More than 13.8 billion years ago, everything that we know was a tiny, subatomic speck. Then, the speck inflated faster than the speed of light in all directions. As inflation slowed, a flood of matter and radiation appeared, creating the Big Bang fireball that allowed for the formation of atoms and molecules and, eventually, stars and galaxies pulled together by gravity. During cosmic inflation, the universe was filled with energy inherent to space itself. This allowed the universe to expand at an exponential rate, with more distant locations moving ever more quickly away. Our observations of the observable universe are consistent with this theory of inflation. The end of inflation is triggered by quantum processes that occur at different times in different places. The regions where inflation ends are thought to pinch off to form a bubble universe. The bubble universe experiences a similar Big Bang and may form a universe like ours. It could also form a universe with entirely different particles and different laws of physics. All bubble universes, including our own continue to grow and are thought to remain separated from other bubble universes because of the space created by continuing inflation. This means no two bubble universes will ever interact or collide, and it's possible that inflation is continuing somewhere in the multiverse.

Another key aspect of parallel universe theories comes from string theory. String theory attempts to explain the entire universe from subatomic particles to the laws of speed and gravity in terms of really small strings that vibrate in 10 or 11 dimensions. String theory allows different bubble universes to have vastly different physical properties, including different types of matter and different laws of physics. When combined with inflation theory, which allows for an unlimited number of bubbles, it provides an explanation for why our universe is so exquisitely well-suited for life.'

Cliff paused a moment. Then continued…

'Now there are four types of parallel universe theories. And they are as follows: Type 1… This type of parallel universe assumes that space is infinite and that the laws of physics always remain the same. Somewhere in this infinite space, there are other planets, solar systems and even galaxies similar to ours, because there is a limited number of ways the same building blocks can arrange themselves. Our "universe" is defined as what humans can currently observe, while any parallel universe would statistically be a great distance away. This parallel universe theory is largely uncontroversial among scientists since many observations and well-supported theories suggest a universe that is immensely large, and perhaps truly infinite. Type 2… This type of parallel universe would allow for regions of space where the basic laws of physics are the same but where there may be different physical constants, different particles and even a different number of dimensions. These universes would arise when cosmic inflation produces different bubble universes. Type 3… This type of parallel universe is where an alternate universe arises from a change that is small… for example, stopping to stroke a cat, or large, for example, taking a job in a different state. The underlying scientific theory arises from an interpretation of quantum mechanics, which is a mathematical description of subatomic particles. Specifically, the "many worlds" interpretation of quantum mechanics states that, for every possible quantum option, there is a universe where that option is realized… for example, leading to one world where you stop to stroke a cat and another world where you do not! Type 4… This type of parallel universe is the most extreme of all, where other universes are governed by completely different physical laws that would be described by completely different mathematical equations. It combines the bubble universes predicted by inflation theory with the vastly different physical properties allowed by string theory.'

Cliff closed the book, his eyes wide. He now began leafing through a thick history book. Thirty minutes passed...

Across the tiled floor a shadow emerged; it broke his focus temporarily. "Cliff what are you doing?" said his wife.

"Reading..." As if crazed, he continued leafing through the pages feverishly, fingering his way around sentences which seemed to tamper with his already broken and confused state of mind. Then he leapt to his feet.

"Sandy, listen to me. I know what I'm about to say may sound crazy, I also know that I'm not suffering from memory loss, in fact, I have a clear vivid recollection of the past 30 years..."

He sat back down, running a shaky hand through his hair.

"It now appears there are other things which don't make any sense. Even historical events are not the way I recall them. Tell me... who is Clark O'Donnell?"

There was an astonished silence, enough to detect the flicker of a heartbeat.

"Are you seriously asking me that?"

"Yes."

"Why, he is the president of the United States and has been for some time."

"Never heard of him. Tell me," he paused regaining his breath. "Was there a Vietnam war?"

"A what war?"

He stood abruptly, walking over to her.

"Sandy, don't you see? There was a war, it did happen. March 8 1965 the first U.S. combat troops arrived in Vietnam and as for this O'Donnell... why I haven't even heard of him."

His face began to contort in horror. Sandy stood motionless.

"Cliff, I really think you need to see someone right away."

"No Sandy, I don't need a doctor. Listen to me. Deep beneath the sea lies a gateway to another world, another dimension, one parallel to our own. In that light-flooded cave I somehow stumbled into it... into this reality."

"I can't believe this. You're insane, totally insane."

She broke down, tears welling in her eyes. Reaching over, he held her in his arms but with a stern shrug, she freed herself from his grip and headed away towards the lounge, helpless and afraid.

A new day began. As the doorbell rang, Cliff awoke, raising his head stiffly from his library desk. At once, the reality of his predicament penetrated his consciousness. Again the doorbell rang, followed by a knock. Bewildered and torn, he made his way over, and from the corner of his eye caught a quick glimpse of Sandy standing quietly mid-way up the spiral staircase, Billy close by. He swung the front door open and sunlight flooded in, stinging his eyes, breaking his morning drowsiness.

"Hi, Cliff. I've brought a friend."

Standing before him was Pete, accompanied by a man dressed in a long dark coat and blue shirt.

"May we come in?"

Cliff's instinctive reaction was to say no but after a few seconds he relented and nodded his head, standing aside to allow Pete to step in, followed by the unknown man, who shut the door behind him.

"Cliff... this is Brad, Brad Stevens."

"Hi Cliff, how are you?" Brad said smiling, gazing at him in sympathetic concern, as if confronting a sick man. Cliff immediately understood the implication from Brad's transparent gesture and tone. Brad then reached out his hand in greeting, but Cliff failed to respond.

"I'm sorry I don't know you... nor do I have any recollection of you... none."

Brad's smile dropped.

"There's no point in this, Pete. I'm telling you, I have never met this man and if you want an explanation, I have one, as incredulous as it may seem."

"Yes, I know, Sandy told me about your theory."

"Not a theory Pete, fact. But I'm looking for a solution, a way out of here, back into my world."

Pete and Brad glanced at each other with worried eyes. Sandy began to inch her way down the stairs, Billy holding onto her anxiously.

"Cliff, listen to me, forget metaphysics, you need medical attention, you are suffering from some kind of neurological condition, a psychotic phase. Stop with this parallel dimension nonsense!"

"No Pete... hear me out. Do I sound like a mad man? Does a mad man speak with such depth, and clarity? That cave, that light catapulted me into an alternate dimension, a parallel dimension, some kind of space time continuum. As I can see, most things around are largely the same, us, streets... but."

"But what!"

"But there are differences like this man Brad. In my world he doesn't exist, at least not to my knowledge. In addition to that, it appears to me that even historical events which I know took place, never occurred here, or if they did, it was somehow different. I spent all night researching."

"Such as..."

"Such as the Vietnam War, it happened alright but the history books don't even mention it... it is nowhere to be found, no record of it whatsoever and as for O'Donnell being the president, never even heard of him! Even the Great Roman Empire, the very one which shaped and built Europe, and transformed our way of thinking for all ages, according to what I read, never existed... Great scientists that made earth shattering inventions are nowhere to be found and are substituted by others which I know never lived."

"Like?"

"Like Enrico Fermi, who started the atomic age. According to the encyclopaedia it was Edward Wilson an American from Washington... list after list of things that just don't add up... a continuity of events that no memory loss could cause nor any mental illness for that matter. I know what I know. In these parallel realities there are differences, some tiny, others major but there are differences. This mysterious dark universe is so complex, made up of atoms, sub-atomic particles, strings of light oscillating with a frequency of which we are all part, a symphony of sounds within a multiverse of parallel dimensions, infinite realities."

"Cliff, listen to yourself," Brad said. "Are you suggesting that the Cliff Fontaine that stands before me, before us, is not the one we have known all these years?"

"Yes, correct. Don't you see that logic would indicate that to be so, there is no other explanation. Clearly you can see that I'm not insane."

"So if that's the case, where is your counterpart?" Pete asked, as if he had now succumbed to the theory. "Where is the other you?"

"I don't know. Perhaps in my world, perhaps in another, who knows, but that's not my problem. If there is a way back, my only chance is to relocate that cave!"

"Stop it! Will you stop?" Sandy cried tearfully. Then impulsively, she ran up the stairs, Billy trailing behind.

In the silence that followed, Cliff began to feel an element of guilt rising within him, but logic told him to push it aside, after all, these people were not who they appeared to be. He meditated, grasping it in its totality, even though he still questioned his sanity. Walking off into the library he sat at his desk, nervous sweat breaking out on his forehead. Moments later he heard the front door open and close, then footsteps approaching. Pete stepped in, sunlight shining across his body as it filtered in through the elegantly curtained window.

"Talk to me Cliff. Brad's gone, it's just you and me."

"What more is there to say? I'm from another world, one where there is another Pete Ellis, one where there's another Sandy and Billy... one where I belong."

His voice faded. Calmly, Pete walked over, and crouched beside him. There was a warm expression on his face, one of acceptance, as if his whole trail of thinking had now switched.

"Cliff, I don't know why but a part of me is beginning to believe you... yet another is telling me you need urgent help. Emotionally I'm being pulled, torn in two separate directions, but because of our friendship, because of my respect for you, as ludicrous as this is…"

He paused, his eyes straying away from Cliff towards the floor, conveying the dilemma he was in.

"We're going back, back out there. If what you're saying is the case, we have no other choice but to find that cave."

Cliff stood up, and walked towards the window where the growing light of day revived him with hope.

"It's my only hope Pete, my only hope."

As darkness approached, they commenced their journey across the tame Pacific waters. Accelerating to maximum speed, Pete navigated ahead in search of the precise location.

"I'm doing my best to relocate the exact spot of your dive, but you do realise it may not be possible?"

Beside him, dressed in his wetsuit, Cliff remained quiet, solely focused on his objective, one which hung in the balance. After all there was no guarantee he could ever escape the clutches of this other world.

"Okay," Pete said, "this will do. It was around here somewhere."

Cliff was unresponsive as he moved over to the side of the boat, staring into the cold waters of the Pacific, trance-like.

"Cliff."

Turning slowly, he gazed at Pete who stood in a luminous yellow jacket. For a time there were no words, yet the muted urgency was plain to see.

"Cliff as bizarre as it is I hope you make it back."

"Me too, Pete... Me too..."

Securing the demand valve around his gums, he bit hard into the rubber, activating his diving torch. Then, with a sharp twist he jumped into the sea, rocking the boat, vanishing below.

He sank through the blackness for a few seconds, then light, bright and fiery engulfed him. In a flash, he found himself staring at his watch inside the cave, the light pulsing and glowing around him as if it were alive. For a moment he fought to maintain consciousness, as the whole scene was almost too much for him to fathom. Briskly, with a snake-like wiggle he swam out, making a quick yet controlled ascent. With his torch his only guide, he could now see the surface drawing closer, the night stars coming into gradual but blurry focus. Pushing a little harder with the aid of his flippers, he was out, out with a splash, sapped dry and lifeless yet his adrenal fix remained. Locating Pete, he attempted to swim over with a series of breaststroke motions, but he couldn't. He paused, solely dependent on his buoyancy compensator to stay afloat.

"Cliff, hold on buddy," Pete yelled, manoeuvring the boat cautiously in his direction.

Cliff's eyes began to close as he gazed up towards the sky in search of refuge. Barely conscious, he caught a glimpse of Pete as he reached out his desperate arms from beyond the boat. But which Pete was it?

A dazzle of light awoke him, as the doctor shone a pencil beam torch into his left eye. He flinched and leapt up acting on impulse, sweating profusely, the dim bed lamp casting a shadow across his sickly face.

"Where am I?"

"It's okay now," the Doctor said warmly. "You're at home, safe."

Cliff lay back, soaking up sweat from his face with his pyjama sleeve. Then, from the doorway, Sandy walked over, her face coming into focus as it met with the dim light of the bedroom. Slowly, reaching out, she held his hand, delicately kneeling beside the bed, her warm perfume filling his nostrils.

"Baby, are you okay?"

"What happened?"

"You were out diving with Pete. Don't you recall? You lost consciousness as you surfaced."

"Yes, that's right," he replied softly, barely moving his lips, Sandy's words acting as a catalyst, to restore his thought process. Gradually, he began to condense his fractured thoughts and broken memories into a semblance of logic. Then, at once, he recalled his predicament.

"Light... that light..."

Sandy stood gazing at the doctor, as if in need of support.

"Light...? What light? What do you mean?" she asked, now staring at Cliff.

The doctor promptly intervened.

"It's okay Mrs Fontaine, he's probably delirious. Rationality at this stage is not to be expected. In a few days he'll be back on his feet, stronger and fitter than ever."

"Thanks Doctor White. Can I see you out?"

"No, I'll be okay. If you need anything just call."

Offering a firm handshake, he smiled, transfusing her with an element of confidence. Swiftly, with briefcase in hand, he left.

Making her way over to the bed, she stood gazing at Cliff worriedly. He was still dazed, but mentally he was piecing together the chain of events like a puzzle. The one vital question that now remained was, had he made it back? The reaction of his wife indicated so, but there was only one real way to find out.

"Sandy, I need to ask something. Please listen to me..."

"Sweetheart, calm down. Let me fix you some hot tea. Give me a couple of minutes."

Now quiet and alone, he gazed around the room almost hoping for some kind of indication, an indication that he was back in his world. Suddenly, the warm silence was shattered by the phone ringing. Reaching over he answered, low and strained, "Yes..."

"Hey Cliff, it's Pete. Are you feeling better? You don't know how relieved I am to hear your voice. I was worried."

For a moment Cliff hesitated, rubbing his hand across his bristled chin. Calculating his words carefully, he replied.

"Yes, I'm feeling okay... but whether I remain that way depends."

"Depends on what?"

"Pete, I need to ask you two questions."

"Go ahead," he said with curiosity.

"Tell me," Cliff's eyes began to switch from left to right, as if he were about to discover the ultimate truth. He took a long deep breath and continued.

"Do I know a Brad Stevens?"

"Who's Brad Stevens?"

Cliff was filled with relief.

"Pete... I know it sounds strange but let me finish. Second question... was there a Vietnam War?"

Pete chuckled to himself, "Yes Cliff there was, it lasted many years. Now are you going to tell me what this is all about?"

"I don't know how to put this. What I'm about to say may shock you. Deep beneath the sea, deep beneath the ocean I found a cave."

"And..."

"And it was like no other. There was a light, a light which shone from it... a light from no apparent source."

"And..."

"Pete, somehow in this cave I stumbled into another world, another dimension, a parallel dimension, one almost identical to this. In that dimension I lived out two days."

"What? Are you serious?"

"Please, you've got to believe me."

"Cliff, I'm sure there's a rational explanation behind it. Remember you were unconscious for some time."

"No Pete, it happened. It was real."

There was a moment of silence.

"Look, this is all a bit bizarre. For now try and get some rest. We'll speak again in the morning, okay?"

"Okay Pete."

Tossing the phone across the bed, Cliff caught the muffled tones of a young girl. Instantly he thought of his son Billy. *'Where was he?'* Sudden panic besieged him. He scanned the wall, looking for that picture, trying to quell a now familiar panic. The door swung open. She ran over. "Dad..."

Terra Unknown

In the mid-day sky, a great shattering roar filled the air. A circle of light sparkled across the planet as they manoeuvred for descent. From the rocket-ship, exhaust valves gushed out clouds of smoke as the jet compressors cooled into silence. Via vocal instruction the hatch door slid open, making contact with the unknown world. Commander Kubo Van den Berg, stepped out, dirt and ash blowing across the view plate of his helmet, his heavy tank weighing him down. Behind, two troopers followed, their grey pressurized gravity-suits glinting in the light.

"What do you think Commander? As expected?"

"Yes, definite signs of some sort of past existence. We've had this planet under observation for sometime but now there's no doubt."

He pointed towards the lifeless landscape, death and ruins everywhere, buildings broken down and half burnt; yellowing remains of structures jutting up from the ground. Across the sky, dark rolling clouds of blackness covered the horizon, grey particles rising and falling. A sombre oppression hung over everything. Around his wrist the rad-detector registered and clicked. Kubo consulted it, taking its atmospheric reading.

"This planet is riddled with radiation. A sign that there may have been a war here... Unreal, how could any civilisation blast themselves out of existence?"

All three looked ahead in silence, desolation and destruction everywhere.

"Doug." He motioned him forward.

"Yes Commander?" acknowledged Doug, lowering the temperature of his suit, kicking debris and rubble from his path.

"Radio in. Tell them we've finally made contact. Some believed we would never make it."

Harris began to fidget nervously, his heavy boots sinking into the dirt below.

"Commander, are we safe here?"

Kubo hesitated, peering into the distance through the rising mist, Harris following his gaze.

"That's something I can't answer right now. That's the chance we take each mission..."

Harris ran his fingers nervously over his cased blast-gun. Kneeling, Doug activated the transmitter on his belt, blowing sharply against the mike. There was a hum then static...followed by a voice, cold, distant and metallic.

"Alpha-3 do you copy? Hello Alpha-3."

Only faint crackling sounds were now audible.

"Commander, I've lost them."

"Don't worry we'll make contact once we're back inside the ship. The communications circuit should be fully operative."

Kubo considered their situation.

"Amazing... our calculations were spot on. This planet is roughly the same size as ours. The gravity field is ideal. The escape velocity will almost be the same as when we left our planet. I knew there would be life. At least there was once."

He smiled with satisfaction.

"Before we leave, we need to activate the suction discs. We have to take back a tank full of atmosphere for testing."

Overhead a winged creature flew past, circling for a time.

"Hey, did you see that?" Harris rasped, pointing.

Kubo gazed up, focusing, watching it go. "I'm sure there are all sorts of living things here. Things beyond our wildest imagination... things which have become immune to the lethal radiation... Any creature alive is obviously well adapted to the environment. The levels of radioactivity are deadly. Practically nothing from our world could exist here."

He caught sight of something glinting in the harsh light on the ground to his left. Kubo knelt, investigating, the others shielding him.

"What is it?" Doug asked rivulets of sweat forming, dripping down the inside face of his helmet.

"A chronological instrument. A device for measuring time..."

Harris's eyes widened.

"Okay, let's head back to the ship," Kubo said, trying to control the tiny tremor in his deep voice. He stood up, dusting his knees. "We need rest. We've had quite a journey. Tomorrow we'll begin our search. We'll cover a six-mile radius. Beyond that..." He paused.

"Beyond that what, Commander...?" Harris questioned.

"Who knows...!"

They turned gazing towards the desolate expanse, the poisonous wind lashing and twisting endlessly across the face of the planet like a tempest and silence, the eternal silence...

Four kilometres out from base the next morning, Harris was waving his scan-com every now and then, in search of alien spy ships. Off to the left a great gaping cavity stretched, deep and dusty. Kubo trudged over through the rubble, halting near the edge, analysing, wondering. From his gloved hand a light shone as he raised it, directing his palm towards the hole. He could see electronic equipment, weapons and highly advanced machinery, grey and bulky. A few creatures rustled and moved, vague indistinguishable shapes in search of refuge.

"What is it?" Doug inquired leaning over his broad shoulder, blast-gun in hand.

"It seems to be some kind of underground quarters. From what I see nothing worth exploring."

"Are you certain?"

"Yes, besides, it won't be easy getting down there."

A broken machine began to hum, partially operative, a complex pattern of lights flashing and alternating with endless combinations. Doug calmly fired at it, a burst of heat blasting out, bursting it apart, springs and components spraying in all directions. He fired again through the mist of particles.

"That should fix it."

"Commander!" Harris yelled. "I can see smoke in the distance."

Through parting mist a fire burned, thick dark smoke ascending.

"Can you see it? There must be someone out there."

"Could be," Kubo replied, unlatching his cased blast-gun, eyes focused. Silently he made a forward command, raising his hand and waving it in a circular motion.

Trudging through the ash with slow calculated steps, they advanced. Then something moved, a furry creature concealing itself in the rubble. Harris fired instinctively. A wave of heat blasted into the atmosphere.

"Damn I missed."

The air was filled with an acrid stench. Again the tiny creature moved, hopping away in a flash.

"Look at it go." Kubo said, "A complex bundle of amino acids... nothing more."

Doug grimaced, imprisoned within the confines of his helmet. The smell of perspiration grew. He turned a dial across his chest regulating the temperature flow of his suit.

"I don't think I can last another moment cooped up in this suit. It's torture."

"Let's push on," Kubo ordered.

Reaching the fire, everything was still, nothing stirred, only sporadic crackles, smouldering fragments. Harris gazed around scanning the landscape, no sound, no motion. They were all on edge. Doug could almost smell his own fear which cut through him like a knife. Ahead on the horizon, he could see a range of mountains, a few rays of sunlight lighting their peaks. Kubo spoke, severing the silence.

"This must have been a small town, look, demolished structures everywhere."

A line of wrecked buildings stretched into the distance. In the centre of the street the ground caved in, its surface covered in stones, and broken glass. A few weeds and plants grew from the ground, multi-coloured blossoms, signs of some kind of remaining life.

"Commander what kind of civilisation lived on this planet?" Harris asked.

"Well, we haven't seen any evidence of the previous inhabitants, nothing but semi-archaeological remains... if that. The war must have occurred sometime ago Harris. All that's left of them is probably organic matter... dust."

"I wonder what they looked like, their physiology, their biological make-up, cell structure, digestive system. Radically different from ours, I'm sure. Fascinates me... What are the chances of finding any alive?"

"None."

"You don't sound optimistic Commander."

There was no reply. A wind began screeching around them spraying dust into the air. The fire flickered feebly, fading slowly. Harris picked up a rusted pipe and began stirring it. The fire hissed spraying sparks around him.

"Hey, look at these long stalks," Doug exclaimed, running his hand around one, assessing. "Some kind of plant life..." It was hard and coarse, like sandpaper. Its leaves dripped with slime. "Who knows, it may be edible but I wouldn't chance it."

The day wore on. Hours passed... They were way out. Ahead stood a large building amazingly untouched, a hard looking structure with no signs of damage. There were no windows, only a door, grey and distinct. Halting in their steps, Doug and Harris watched the surroundings while Kubo considered their next move.

"Strange, the one and only structure still standing in its entirety. Must be of importance... built from special alloys. Perhaps bomb proof."

Kubo walked over alone, trudging cautiously until he reached the building. Fatigue set in, his legs burned with lactic acid, stiffening. With a heavy hand he pushed at the door, but it wouldn't budge. Then, reaching for his blast-gun he moved back a few steps and fired. The door stood firm, repelling the impact. Finally, he activated his laser-torch, in an attempt to burn through it. Again, it stood firm.

"Doug... Harris," he yelled. "I'll have to use a D-Bomb. This door won't open."

Moving back at a set distance, Kubo unfastened a disc from his belt, unscrewing the cap and locking it into place. Squatting, with a wave he signalled to the others to take position. They knelt, heads down, eyes closed. Kubo calculated the trajectory, gazing at the door, his face tense, his mind focused. Then in swift motion, he threw the disc-bomb. It sailed through the air, hitting the ground, bouncing and rolling until it halted beside the target. Suddenly, it exploded, blowing the door apart. A wave of hot air rushed over their heads, shrapnel flying in all directions, dust and ash. Underfoot faint vibrations shot through the ground, but apart from the door, the structure stood, absorbing the aftershock. They waited, watching the dust fade. The door was gone, dissolved into particles.

Suddenly a robot leapt out from the clouds of ash, its mechanical photocell eyes yellow and luminous. Swiftly, Harris opened his blast-gun, slid a fresh round of ammunition into place, snapped it shut and pointed. Running his finger over the trigger, he stood firm, took aim, and fired. The beam connected, blowing the robot apart, wires, springs, and circuits flying into the air. All activity from it ceased, its luminous eyes fading, winking until there was no movement. Its elongated steel jaw hung open, exposing tiny intricate components.

Kubo walked over, the others following behind. Pausing to make sure it was completely inactivated, he eventually knelt, studying it intently, prodding into the gaping beam hole across its chest. Although inert, tiny wheels continued to spin, miniature components labouring, feebly operating. With a finger he touched the motor circuit. Its half-blown arm swung aside.

"This is one complex bundle of machinery, very similar to the ones constructed back home. Probably used during the war, hopefully it's the last..."

Kubo gazed towards the building, dust now settling around the jagged opening.

"Be prepared... there may be more."

Stepping inside, they paused. Splattered across the ground was a line of robots, some already victims of the corrosive process. At the far end of the room an illuminated board hung, mathematical diagrams drawn across it in yellow. Dangling wall charts covered every inch of vertical space.

There was a series of dark corridors, long and narrow. Down a selected passage they walked curiously, slowly, until they reached a metal door. Doug pushed and kicked at it, but it wouldn't open. Reaching for his laser-torch he burnt a neat circular hole, wide enough to pass through. Kubo motioned him forward with his finger. Doug stepped in, blast-gun in hand, Harris pressing behind.

"It's clear Commander." Doug barked... the relief in his voice evident. "Nothing but large wooden boxes... some kind of cargo..."

Kubo stepped in, walking around the large dusty room. Across the ceiling, he noticed a long, broken half dangling wire. Underfoot, bits of broken glass crunched. Suddenly, three robots rushed into the room like insects, holding beam-rifles.

"Freeze," one rasped metallically.

In a frenzy of panic, Doug and Harris fired, blowing the robots out of existence. All that remained were bits of metal, bundles of twisted metallic shell, wheels, bolts rolling into silence. Even sections of the walls had been penetrated, eaten away, gaping jagged holes billowing with smoke unveiling the outside world.

Doug bent down and twisted a beam-rifle from one of the robot's clenched humanoid hands. Standing up, he gazed at it, running his fingers over the smooth metal.

"Interesting weapon."

"What do you think are in these boxes Commander?" Harris asked, beating his fist against one, raising dust from the rough wooden lid.

"Whatever it is, feel free to take. Remember we are legally authorised to bring back anything of use. It was agreed by the galactic trade conference... signed and sealed before this mission..."

Harris slid one open, placing the lid onto the ground. There was an odour of age and dust. He took out his scanning device...

"Minerals, metals, substances, a whole selection from various planets in our solar system. Looks like whatever or whoever lived here were pirates." Harris shrugged stoically.

Kubo moved over and peered inside. "Pirates indeed! Don't you recognize these marks?" He pointed. "These mineral deposits and metals were stolen from us many years back during the galactic mining projects. He glanced around. The whole shipment..."

"Oh yeah," Doug said reflectively. "There were several riots back home. It went down on the file as missing... nothing more."

"That's right. Without these materials we would never have had temperature alternating buildings, even our advanced control equipment inside the ship depends on it in order to operate smoothly, effectively."

Kubo placed his hand inside, touching and turning.

"Bronomite," he smiled thinking back. "That's what they use in customs checks back home, in order to get the truth from suspicious voyagers. In dangerously high doses they can even use it to determine if a person is criminally minded and what types of crime he or she may plan in the future. It almost has a way of looking into future events that may or may not happen, by detecting people's desires, plans, and tendencies."

He continued to explore inside the box.

"Menzite... used in our vid-screens to create a 4-d effect. Dolaphite, used in medicine... Helps fight against many forms of disease."

He was caught in nostalgic thought.

"They've even got hold of Kronian. The Kronian mines of Arcadon." He recalled the wars and riots there with the locals, distant but real images, scenes and sensations.

"What's it used for?" Doug inquired.

"Aptitude testing apparatus... virtuosity... With it we can determine what occupation is best suited for us measuring our intellect, and abilities. Kronian testers are used extensively all round, especially for recruiting Troopers."

Kubo paused then continued.

"We have enough of these supplies to last us twenty generations and more but that doesn't allow for pirates invading... passing into prohibited zones unlawfully." He clenched his fist in anger.

"When we get back, we'll determine whether or not it's worth mining here for natural resources. Who knows what lies beneath us."

"Hey, do you hear that, Commander?"

"Hear what Doug?"

"That sound. Wait... Listen!"

Alerted, Harris nodded in disturbed agreement.

There was a ticking sound, constant but faint. An alarm rattled. They glanced at each other.

"Quick, let's get out of here," Kubo commanded urgently.

Rapidly working their way through the narrow corridor, they exited the building. At a set distance, they dived for cover. In a flash the building exploded into a shapeless mass of rubble, smoke, fire and debris littering and lighting up the mid-afternoon sky. Kubo turned back in horror, his dirt-streaked view plate partially masking his sight. A spiralling dark cloud formed, unleashing toxic fumes into the already radioactive atmosphere.

"That was close," Kubo muttered with relief. "Let's return to base."

The sun had set, and the world was dark and still, creatures seeking refuge amongst the rubble and ash, a few stars glinting above, escaping through the dense clouds of ash.

Outside the rocket-ship, Doug and Harris sat on a couple of rocks talking softly. Kubo paced back and forth contemplating the day's events, his helmet-beam activated and bright. He flicked on his suit heater and continued, the helmet-beam cutting into the night darkness and lighting up a piece of jagged metal ahead of him. The scan-com on Harris' belt suddenly flashed red, bleeping. Crouching on one knee, Harris lifted it from his belt, waving it into the air. Across the small screen, a spy ship was displayed, sleek, slender and aerodynamic. Rapidly, the ship descended, landing lights flickering on and off, brake jets igniting a fiery red.

As it touched down, making contact with the surface of the planet, Harris reduced magnification, acquiring a multi-dimensional view of the surroundings, as well as the ship itself. He watched intently for motion and sound. Neither came.

"Do you recognize it? One of ours?"

"No Commander." He turned the screen in his direction, enlarging the image of the ship. G-7 was marked across its slender frame.

"Doug, prepare to fire. Mark it down on the system as an illegal entry. Don't forget."

"Okay."

"What are the coordinates at present?

Harris took a reading.

"Eleven kilometres north-east."

"Commander which gun do I activate, laser or vapour?"

"There's a strong night wind. Considering the distance the vapour may lose its trajectory, and even then, by the time the corrosive action takes place, they could escape. Use laser."

Before they could fire, the ship lifted, spiralling into the atmosphere, its rapid movement causing the scan-com to lose track.

"It's gone," Harris complained, the glare of the scan-com reflecting across the glass view plate of his helmet. "It's as if they heard us whatever they were."

It hovered for a time, stalking the skies, moving above a range of mountains and then disappeared into outer space, tearing through the planet's gravitational field at terrifying speed, severing the gravitational umbilical cord. The screen went blank. The red warning light deactivated, fading to green.

"All clear Commander."

"Good, let's get some rest. Tomorrow we'll head out there. We need to investigate."

Kubo stood alone for a time, gazing up into the sky as if for confirmation, the cold nocturnal stars now sliding in and out of a foggy mist. The planet was cooling off. Then he caught sight of an object, a meteor, soon to be burnt up in the atmosphere. He turned, heading towards the ship.

The night was passing rapidly, another day emerging... the dark fading into grey, the landscape slowly forming and taking shape in the growing light. Sunrise was beautiful, dimly masked by particles in suspension.

At the top of a hill, nine kilometres out from base, Kubo could see the remains of a space-station, beyond it a city, gleaming white ruins scattered here and there.

"Commander," Doug pointed indicating east. "That's where the ship landed."

Kubo halted regaining his breath, theorising, thinking.

"An old space-station."

He scanned the remains. There were heaps of metal and rubble. Cosmic-crafts were few, and those that remained were clearly inoperative, metal fatigue and structural damage clearly evident even from a distance.

"Move on."

With the space-station meters away they discovered that beneath them lay an underground base, a semi-corroded metallic ladder leading down to it.

"Doug... Harris, see what you can find up here. Report back within twenty minutes. I'm going down."

As Kubo descended, his boots clattered and echoed against the rusted metal of the ladder. Step by step he made his way down. Reaching the bottom, he stumbled backwards, promptly regaining equilibrium. His back ached, a dull constant ache. The ground was wet, the underground base tubular in design. Robots lay motionless, broken in sections of decaying metal, beam-rifles and glass everywhere. There were rooms, generators, complex apparatus and wall charts of cosmic-crafts with listed destinations. Moving towards a dark room the beam from his helmet activated, cutting a white circular path in front of him. Across the ground he noticed sand

and two long snaking wires. Squatting, he traced them to where they connected to a black machine, clearly no longer functional. Then, deep in thought, he picked up a handful of sand letting it trickle through his gloved fingers. After a few moments, he moved out.

Working his way back up, he reached the surface, the desolate landscape engulfing him through the mist and ash. Rain began to fall, drenching the alien planet in torrents of water. Turning a dial around on his belt, a small tube extended from within the helmet, directing nutrition capsules into his mouth. He swallowed. Then from his tank, he pulled out the exhausted tube which carried the capsules, tossing it to the ground. Five remained, plenty to last him a week or more, the difference between life and death.

Cautiously he pushed on, debris crunching under him. Suddenly he tripped on something metallic, most of it concealed beneath the rubble and dirt.

Bending, he fought to retrieve it, gripping his hands around the exposed edge. Slowly he slid it out and stood gazing at a large rusty telescope. A symbol was imprinted across it, nothing more. Then his transmitter bleeped into life. He blew against the mike...

"Commander it's Harris, do you copy?" His voice came in distantly.

"Yes, I copy."

A moment of wave interference... The rain increased, swirling with the wind.

"I just received telemetry for that G-7 craft, the one we caught on the scan-com. They claim to be the only remaining survivors from this planet. There are six of them." His voice began to fade, fading with breathless accomplishment.

"Planet Earth Commander, that's the name of this planet. That's what they told me. The creatures describe themselves as humans, humans, Commander! They are returning to their new home as we speak... the Moon, Earth's only natural satellite. They have been living on the Moon for some time in a huge indoor dome."

Kubo clicked off the transmitter gazing up, breathing in the controlled atmosphere. "Earth, humans, pirates," he muttered. "What other surprises lie ahead on this semi-abandoned death planet?"

Destination CITON

Stripping the winning lotto numbers from his weekly journal, Ed Rutherford dashed to the vid-phone consumed with elation. Instantly his mind lit up with images of new worlds, along with the reality that Earth would no longer be home. Speaking into the phone, he blasted out the three-digit number and was immediately connected. After a few beeps, a voice spoke, a face forming on the vid-screen simultaneously.

"Solar Voyages."

Gripped with an overwhelming excitement, he moved his lips soundlessly, struggling to form words. Then composing himself, he replied, almost stuttering, "Yes, good morning. I've won, I have the winning numbers."

His green eyes sparkled, and he hopped from foot to foot awaiting his prize. The invisible flame deep within him that had diminished over the years had suddenly reignited.

"Identity code please," the soft feminine voice chirped.

He read out the embedded code on the palm of his left hand, becoming impatient with the formalities.

Silently, briskly, the lady registered the data, her face on the vid-screen now concealed in waves of visual static.

"Mr Ed Rutherford of 9, Olympia Drive, Los Angeles..."

"Yes, that's me," he murmured excitedly, running his tongue around the edges of his mouth.

"Ok! Well congratulations Sir! You should make your way over to head office as soon as you can. The address is imprinted on the back of the winning digits."

Almost dizzy with euphoria, he clicked off the vid-phone, swigged down a celebratory shot of warm whisky and headed for the door.

At the L.A hover-station, he awaited his train impatiently, oblivious to the world around him, his hands deep inside his coat pockets battling the chill. People, noise and restless chaos engulfed him, filling virtually every corner. A sudden wink of blue light from a forming hologram listing climatic data caught his attention dragging him back to the world of reality, a reality that suddenly had a tinge of the surreal. Then, his vc-watch buzzed. With idle concern, he lifted his wrist to his mouth covering the small screen with his hand, blocking out the visual portion of the transmission.

"Hello."

"Ed where are you? You were supposed to be at work an hour ago."

"Can't make it... Talk later. Got to go...!"

With a great deal of satisfaction, he deactivated the connection with the turn of a dial. He was in no mood for dialogue especially with his boss. *'There's no need to interact with him anymore,'* he thought and then chuckled to himself. For a moment, he pictured him, a tall lanky, bald, and intimidating figure of a man who vented his life's frustrations and deep insecurities on others. Ed just happened to be his favourite daily victim, it was nothing personal.

Moments later the hover-train arrived, its rusty metallic frame reflecting the bright overhead station lights. As the doors opened with a swish, a whole crowd of bodies hurtled into the opening, squeezing and pushing their way through, battling for the few remaining seats. Ed was able to remain calm for once. After all he had just won the greatest prize, a one-way trip to a mystery paradise planet... a distant sphere faraway in another galaxy where life would be radically different. Only the mega rich and famous inhabited the other worlds. Most of the population, the masses, could only dream of such an idea and longed for it in envy. '*A low paid vehicle salesman like me?*' he thought to himself, '*it's a miserable, dull, grey life to be sure*. But all that was about to change...

Walking up to a towering skyscraper within the confines of the densely populated city centre, a melting pot of cultures, Ed pushed his way through the glass doors with ease, butterflies with jack boots dancing in his stomach. With a quick glance he located the reception area, where a chubby security guard sat half dazed with boredom, flicking through a creased news journal. He forced a smile, as Ed rushed over.

"Good day, how can I help?"

"I've come to make my claim."

"Well congratulations!" The envy in the guard's voice was unmistakeable. "Make your way to the thirtieth floor, Sir, and take the brown door to your right."

Ed almost skipped across the foyer but as he waited for the elevator doubt dampened his sense of euphoria. Was this all a joke? Good fortune like this never visited him. The chances of this happening were so astronomically low, there must have been a mistake. In a few minutes he would be sent away with his tail between his legs, back to his mundane, boring unfulfilled reality, only now, it would be ten times worse… and he'd have to try and get his job back. The ride to the thirtieth floor calmed him. Why shouldn't he be this lucky. He had no one, asked no one for anything, owed nothing to nobody. He was due a bit of luck.

As the express elevator came to a halt, Ed walked out with a spring in his step, his excitement restored. He headed towards a large brown door where a bright glowing sign demanded his attention, '*Solar Voyages*.' Adjusting his sandy blond hair, he was about to press the buzzer, but before he could move, the door slid open. Standing before him was a dynamic looking man, in his thirties wearing a distinctive green bow tie.

"Clark O'Bryan. You must be Mr Rutherford!"

He extended his slender hand in greeting. They shook, then after a moment of hesitation, Ed found his voice again.

"Yes, yes I am." A huge grin began to spread across his face.

"Please Mr Rutherford come this way."

After a brisk walk down a long corridor filled with sound and activity, he was led into a large office. Barely containing his excitement, Ed placed the strip of winning lotto numbers on the desk then sat in a grey swivel chair, biting at the edges of his mouth in expectancy. Across the wall a vid-com suddenly flashed, a red and green light which constantly alternated, followed by a ping and then another.

"Excuse me," Mr O'Bryan said, strolling over to the vid-com. "Yes…" There was a rapid exchange of words, no more than a few seconds, the call terminating quickly. Then, he took the luminous strip of winning digits, gazed at them for a time and started to walk purposefully to the back of the office towards a D-UNIT; a compact piece of machinery that extended from the floor midway to the ceiling. Standing before it, he punched in the numbers with deliberation. Ed's face formed digitally on the screen in a three-dimensional format. Having completed its mobile phases the machine shut down, now visually inoperative. There was a brief pause. With a sharp turn he walked over towards Ed smiling.

"Congratulations Sir, I can now confirm that you are the luckiest man alive and that's not just a figure of speech. From the records, I see that this was your very first entry and you won straight off. It almost defies the laws of probability. We have one annual winner. You Sir, are our lucky number five."

Ed leapt up gripping the man's hand. He had only entered the lotto once, a few days back, a spontaneous half-hearted decision after a terrible day at work with nothing to come home to and now he was about to step into a world of luxury and unimaginable adventure.

"Thanks… I can't believe it myself. When do I leave?"

"First things first, Mr Rutherford. Please, sit down."

Ed fell back into the chair.

"I'm sure you're longing to know where your awaited destination is."

Ed unable suddenly to speak, urged him on with his eyes, moistening his lips.

"But before I satisfy your curiosity, I need to clarify one little factor."

There was a brief silence. Ed's anxiety rose to fever-pitch.

"You must understand Mr Rutherford, that under no circumstances can anyone join you... it's for you alone. This applies irrevocably to all, unless married."

For a loner like Ed this news wasn't going to cause any waves or turbulent feelings, after all, he had only himself to worry about, no friends, no family, only associates. It was ideal.

"Shall we continue?"

Ed nodded in agreement, locking his fingers and cracking his knuckles.

"Your destination is Citon, Galaxy Andromeda, 2.2 million-light years away, the nearest neighbouring large galaxy."

"I knew... I knew it." Ed blurted out. "Tell me, is it really that beautiful?"

Mr O'Bryan's eyes lit with assurance. "Yes of course Sir, it's the place where dreams are made of. Of all the planets Citon is very special. You're a fortunate man."

Adjusting his bow tie, he sat down on the other side of the desk and then continued, "The landscape of this marvellous planet is diverse, to say the least. There are mountains, lakes, rivers, endless verdant fields which stretch as far as the eye can see... not to mention a wide variety of animal life." He paused.

"Go on," Ed urged in his excitement.

"There are two suns perpetually shining... two giant heat radiating orbs. In the evening the temperature lowers radically, but it's certainly no colder than here. There is also an incredible variety of plant life found nowhere else in the galaxy."

Sweat broke out across Ed's forehead. He could barely contain himself as his mind began building images around these words.

"And the house?"

"You will be living in a mansion exactly one mile from the nearest centre where there are shops, restaurants, bars and all the other evening entertainment spots which will fulfil your day and nocturnal desires, with unlimited credits to spend."

Ed smiled, absorbing the information, greedily assimilating the facts.

"Now, your departure date... how soon do you want to leave? It's totally your choice."

Ed's expression signalled his intent before he could get the words out.

"I'll leave tomorrow."

"Great. Make your way to the spaceport by ten tomorrow morning and one of our reps will meet you."

In the idle hours of dawn, and before his bed alarm could ring, some inner reflex... his trip... the numbers... something, disturbed his sleep. He awoke, slowly opening his eyes and assembling his scattered thoughts. He slipped out of bed and stretched. The image of Citon flashed in his mind dissolving his morning drowsiness, bringing an uncustomary smile to his face. It wouldn't be long now before he saw the alien world in all its beauty and splendour. Raising his arm he checked the time as the morning sunlight shone across his face.

Then leaning over towards the vid-phone by the side of his bed, he dialled for a hover-cab. The arrival time was displayed across the screen almost instantly; twenty minutes was all he had. In a quick and coordinated burst of activity, he dashed towards his cupboard and began changing into some fresh clothes. Of course there was no need to pack anything, he was about to commence a whole new, fresh, chapter in his life. The few items that he owned like clothes, a small desk, etc... were not needed. Those items could all be left behind. He would take nothing from his old, dismal life. He owed nothing to the landlord. All the payments had been made. He wasn't going to even bother calling to explain anything. He would just leave without saying a word. He was too excited.

Within no time he was airborne, inside the hover-cab, flying above the skyscrapers of downtown LA, blending in with the endless tide of air-vehicles. Below he could vaguely distinguish human life, as the faint images of people and surface-vehicles moved around in a circuitry of motion. "Earthly existence... what a pain and struggle, but not anymore," he muttered softly.

The hover-cab began a gliding descent; the world was approaching fast. After a smooth landing, aided by anti-gravity technology, he paid the driver by swiping his hand before the credit-reader and then stepped out, gazing at the huge spaceport which stood before him, shimmering in the sun. Then from seemingly nowhere, a crew of reporters circled around him. Before he had time to digest the scene, a trans-cord device was shoved up to his gaping mouth. He took a step back, wondering where they had come from, how they had known and trying to make sense of the cacophony.

"Sir, please tell our global viewers how it feels to be this year's lucky lotto winner."

The crew drew closer, a few tourists turned and muttered to each other in awe and admiration. Ed was suddenly gripped with a sense of destiny. A mere chance in a billion, picking those seven winning digits had propelled him to stardom. The game of chance had paid off. Standing there in reflected glory he tried to compose himself, battling to find words appropriate to his sudden star-like image. All eyes focused on him. He gesticulated and then spoke into the device.

"There are no words to describe it... none," he said with an almost ironic tone.

"Is it true that you only entered the lotto once and won it straight off?"

"Yes indeed. I can't believe it myself, really. That's all I have to say."

With flushed cheeks he edged his way through the crew of reporters and headed directly for the entrance of the spaceport. A female rep from Solar Voyages was waiting for him.

"Mr Rutherford, I'm Marianne Lee, I trust you are all set to go?"

"Yes", he answered, his eyes straying away timidly, gazing at a large travel-screen which displayed its usual holiday package deals. He refocused.

"Please Sir, if you'll come with me?"

He followed without replying, his eyes and mind elsewhere. Walking past the converging crowds he was led to a doorway. Security guards stood either side, dressed in their familiar pale blue uniforms.

"Congratulations, Sir," the one to the left muttered tipping his cap.

Ed grinned and with a nod of his head accepted the guard's kind words. As the doors slid apart, they stepped through, a row of yellowish lights marking the way. Cold air circled around them. His heartbeat began to increase. At the far end of the hall sat the latest transportation mechanism, which only the mega rich and government agents could afford, a revolutionary teleport operating homeostatically, without human attention. It sat there, luminous and inviting, and appeared to absorb light rather than reflect it.

Gazing at it, Ed began to feel a little apprehensive. Pointing over he said, "I've heard all about this new machine, but how reliable is it?"

The woman smiled, registering his concerns.

"Sir, people spend millions of credits on this daily. You can be sure that it is the most reliable transportation mechanism in the world. The wealthy don't take chances with their well-being. However, it's not unusual to feel a touch nervous, especially if it's your first time. It is the only way you can travel to other galaxies with instantaneous effect. Come let me explain."

They walked over to it and then halted, Ed recapturing some of his lost composure.

"Within a matter of seconds you will find yourself on Citon at the spaceport. The process is simple. You will be disassembled and then reassembled very quickly. As I'm sure you are aware, we are a cluster of atoms, particles. This device breaks up the atomic structure, in this case yours, stores it, and then reassembles it in mathematical order, at the set destination. There is another form of teleportation that we do use sometimes where basically, you scan the object in one place and just transmit the instructions for how to reassemble it somewhere else using different molecules and atoms. In short, your body is scanned, and the information is transmitted somewhere else and used to build an entirely new body out of different materials. This process, the scan-and-reassemble type of teleportation is actually possible thanks to a property of quantum mechanics called, quantum entanglement. Quantum entanglement occurs when two or more particles are forced to hold mutually exclusive states, so determining one simultaneously determines the other."

Ed stood there impressed. Although completely lost, he thought he had a grasp of the general idea.

"Are you ready Mr Rutherford?" she said soothingly.

He nodded. Walking over into a circle of flickering lights, he stood, calm and collected. Around him the machine came to life, as if it were a living entity in its own right. With the click of a switch, the lady released a lever which in turn caused a humming sound, indicating a flow of energy. Above Ed's head, a fiery beam of white light fell, consuming him into nothingness. In a flash his image reappeared, materialising into existence. Opening his eyes he found himself standing in front of a young man. From his attire alone, Ed knew he was in another world. The man lowered his hat in greeting, yet something in his keen glance troubled Ed.

"Welcome to Citon, I'm your host, Neo." He smiled.

Ed returned the seemingly fabricated smile. Gazing around at the well-lit hallway, he could almost sense the alien world that lay beyond the confines of the spaceport. It reminded him that he was light years from Earth.

"Mr Rutherford, shall we commence our journey to your new home?

"Yes, absolutely!" he replied eagerly, shaking off his doubts. Without further dialogue, the man turned and started to walk slowly towards the end of the long hall, Ed pressing close behind. As they approached the door it appeared to melt away. Once they were through, it reformed quickly. Striding through the semi-empty spaceport they came to the exit, where a neon sign flashed in red, '*Welcome to Citon.*' For a brief moment, the whole experience felt remarkably familiar. Somewhere in the back of his mind it echoed, he could almost recall it, but how? Perhaps somewhere in his dreams...? With a shrug of his shoulders, he dismissed the subject without further probing.

Exiting the spaceport, he gazed into the hazy mid-afternoon alien sky. It was captivating and brilliant. Suspended in the distance, like two giant eyes were the suns diffusing an unearthly light, and the land for miles appeared to shimmer and glow majestically. He jumped as he suddenly felt something alive staggering over his thumb, an alien life form, tiny and yellow, ant-like. Intrigued, he watched its movements as it amazingly appeared to mutate and alter its colour.

He brushed it gently away watching it fall and disappear into the dry grey soil below. That moment proved decisive. It catapulted him from his child-like approach to one more serious and questioning; the psychological transition was instant. What a sudden twist of fate! His whole life had swung from one of emptiness to this, all because of one spontaneous decision, one which had paid off handsomely. But what was it that motivated him to enter the lotto? How was it possible to win straight off? He probed his mind in search of logical answers to the bizarre sequence of events and improbabilities that led to his present success... none enlightened him, it was futile. Instead, he savoured the moment, taking in his first deep breath of alien air. This was now home.

Walking over to an air-vehicle, the host pulled out a small sensitive control gadget from his pocket and began manipulating the dials. The doors of the vehicle opened slanting upwards, and its anti-gravity operating mechanism came to life. Steadily and maintaining equilibrium, they ascended into the sky, hovering above the planet's equator. Leaning over to one side Ed admired the beauty down below. The bird's eye view was spectacular, revealing an almost earth-like environment, filled with lakes and rivers like liquid silver, an ocean, mountains, endless green fields, yet there was a peculiar haze in the atmosphere and the two scorching suns conspired to remind him that he was indeed in another galaxy.

Reaching the ground, the air-vehicle came to a halt. Ed quickly slid the door open and stepped out onto the stony ground. Through the soles of his shoes he could feel vibrations that signified life and activity. Then he noticed that directly in front of him, stood a mansion which had an almost liquid crystal hue to it, a peculiar grey with a network of leaves and branches covering a small section. Surrounding it in all directions were beautiful fields abounding with colourful plants the likes of which he had never seen, broken occasionally by tall white gleaming buildings, some pyramid shaped, others vertical and narrow. Turning his head towards his host, he raised his hand and pointed at the mansion.

"That's mine?"

"Yes Mr Rutherford, that's yours," the man replied.

Ed was captivated by its elaborate design; the whole experience had somewhat numbed him of emotion but fresh energy stirred within him. Waving his hand before the code beam, the plush white doors slid apart, retracting into the walls for concealment. Ed stepped in, his host following behind.

"So Mr Rutherford, is it to your liking?"

With a sharp turn he replied. "To my liking...? Yes, yes, it is."

His voice trailed away, his mind now engaged in deep thought. Again a wave of fascinated awe swept through him. Then that feeling of familiarity gripped him again, pestering his mind. Even the air had a nostalgic scent to it, but he still couldn't quite pinpoint nor equate what it was. He scanned the surroundings, the light pink sofa, the vision-screen, the stone floor; everything was pleasing and inviting.

"Well, Mr Rutherford," his host exclaimed, "I'll leave you to it and give you some time to adjust." From his pocket, he pulled out a complex looking device, placing it into Ed's palm.

"Here, if you need anything you can dial a hologram from this."

Tipping his hat politely he left, the doors sliding back into place, cutting off the faint sounds and muffled echoes from outside. Alone and tired, Ed paced about. Through a curtained window he caught a glimpse of the town, distant shapes of people and life. He could vaguely distinguish a line of tall hard structures, but the bright haze concealed most of it. Striding towards the kitchen he paused at the entrance, dutifully activating the device. Immediately a hologram appeared, taking on the form of a young man.

"Welcome Mr Rutherford, please make your requests known."

Ed laughed. *'Interesting toy,'* he thought, tossing it into the air and catching it. Everything was perfect, almost too perfect. With the turn of a dial the hologram faded, blurring and twisting into an oscillating haze and then nothingness. Placing the device down on the translucent kitchen-table, he strolled back into the lounge, where he sank into the sofa. He sighed. He felt tired, yet mentally lucid.

Then, midway to the ceiling, he spotted something he hadn't initially noticed. He scratched his head curiously, gazing up at a machine that suddenly sparked into life. It discharged an array of sounds like rebounding radar signals at an unusual frequency, and then began to descend towards him slowly, guided and manipulated by mechanical arms. He adjusted himself, sitting rigid as the machine halted before him. It became apparent it was some sort of vision-set, silver and bulky, unlike the one in the corner of the room. The screen came alive and a computer-animated male face formed. Via an audio system current passed from transformer to speaker, and a mechanical voice suddenly droned, "Sebastian."

Ed sat back baffled, anxious eyes igniting with confusion. Although the name was unknown to him, it seemed to have a strange kind of significance. Again the voice spoke and said, "Sebastian."

"Who are you?" Ed demanded nervously.

"There is a technical error. Your time here has now expired."

"What! What are you talking about?" He paused. '*This is ridiculous*,' Ed thought, '*I've only just arrived here.*' Before he could think any further, the machine replied.

"Actually you have been here quite some time."

"Wait a minute, I never spoke."

"Indeed you didn't."

"Hey what kind of game is this?" Ed shouted, defiant in his attitude, his anxiety building. "How did you read my mind?"

Ed began to realise something was desperately wrong. '*Machines couldn't read people's thoughts, could they?*' he wondered. Moving towards the machine in fascination, he began to touch and prod his way around in search of answers, his face working spasmodically.

"Sebastian!"

He leapt back mystified and replied, pointing at the face on the screen, "Why do you keep calling me that, I'm Ed?"

There was no immediate reply, only silence met the convoluted echoes of his mind. '*Maybe Sebastian was the previous owner. What had happened to him?*' Ed wondered nervously. An interval passed in which the machine appeared inoperative. Taking in a breath of air, Ed began to regain a measure of calm, almost as if he was resigning himself to the fact that a sinister reality awaited. His eyes were focused, fixed on the screen.

The machine then suddenly announced, "Due to a technical malfunction I'm afraid I have to inform you of the truth. You are not Ed Rutherford."

Ed laughed, but there were ripples of fear and tension in his voice. Something deep inside him, hidden and subdued, recognised the truth of these words but he refused to acknowledge it and challenged the machine.

"So who am I then?"

"You are Sebastian Eckardt, an interplanetary spy."

"Really," Ed replied sarcastically. "Sure. Me a spy...? Of course...!"

"You see Sebastian, everything that you see, and feel is fabricated... a virtual world. You yourself decided to have the virtual journey implanted in your head in order to escape the reality of your incarceration on Citon. Unfortunately, that implantation has proved unsuccessful."

"What implantation?" he yelled out abruptly.

"The one that you requested."

"Are you telling me that I'm living in a simulated world, and that nothing around me is real... including myself?" He banged his fist against the arm of the sofa to emphasize his point.

"Precisely," the screen flashed its reply.

"So, if that's the case, you're not real either?"

"Incorrect, I am very real. I am a highly advanced program inside your head guiding you out of fantasy into reality."

Ed was gripped by that odd familiar feeling, the one which had haunted him since his arrival. He was totally immobile.

"You see Sebastian, after your sentence three months ago on Earth, you were immediately sent to Citon via a teleportation device. You were given two options: To live out the remainder of your life on this abandoned hazardous planet, facing the daily deadly realities with hundreds of other criminals, until death found you, or to live on this hazardous planet, strapped to a highly advanced machine where you would live out a virtual trip of your choice, the one implanted in your head where you took on a whole new identity. You chose Ed Rutherford, the low paid vehicle salesman who had just won the lotto and was about to embark on a new life on the paradise planet Citon. But the truth is Citon is nothing more than a death planet, nothing like the virtual trip is portraying."

"Wait a minute," Ed said leaping to his feet, "let's get this straight. How do you explain all my memories since childhood? Are they all virtual too?"

"They are nothing more than false implants, an artificial construct. During the implantation your true memory bank was erased, along with your identity. All past events, every single memory and emotion you experienced as Ed Rutherford are false."

Ed fell back into his seat caught in a web of confusion and terror. It all felt too real, everything so tangible. Even the mundane scent of his body was too real to question. Then regaining his composure he spoke to the machine again.

"So, why have you chosen to reveal all of this to me now? Explain in full! And how long have I been like this, living in this virtual world?"

Again the computerized voice replied, "I have already told you that due to a technical malfunction I've had to inform you of the truth; that is, you are not Ed Rutherford. Additionally it is important for you to know that you were supposed to live out your life in this delusionary world of Ed Rutherford to the full, while the real you, Sebastian Eckardt, slowly withered away and eventually ceased to be. I am programmed to reveal all to you in the case of an unfortunate event such as this technical malfunction. With regards to the time period, you have been in this virtual world three months. As soon as you arrived here on Citon, you were taken to a chamber by officials and strapped to a highly advanced machine where you should have lived out this virtual trip."

"That can't be."

"It is futile to compare time lapses between reality and fantasy. There is no sense of chronology attached."

The voice now became slow, muffled, distant and metallic.

"Soon you will awaken from this virtual world..."

Suddenly, there was a sound, a ticking sound which appeared to come from out of nowhere. The sound grew louder, almost deafening. Covering his ears with his hands, Ed was gripped in immobilizing fear. Then, from the machine, a beam of light followed in a wave, passing above Ed's head, fading moments later. Then it entered the most complex part of its cycle as the program reached its final phase of operation.

"What's happening to me?" Ed yelled.

At that precise moment, as if it had been deactivated, the sunlight was no more. He looked up with a startled gaze. All he could see were undefined objects twisting and fading, expanding and retracting then collapsing into a vacuum of space and obscurity. Everything that surrounded him was obliterated by a deepening blackness which swirled around him, yet oddly the animated figure across the screen remained intact, brighter and more real than before. Reaching out he tried to touch it, the only seemingly tangible object that now remained in his universe, but that too soon faded into a shapeless mass of non-existence. Then darkness, total darkness...

Suddenly he jerked awake, his blurred eyes registering reality. Instinctively he scrabbled at his face, ripping off the mask which was connected via a trailing wire to a black bulky machine. It was functioning at maximum capacity, monitoring his respiration and heart rate via stethoscopic sensors, registering his body temperature which was displayed across a screen in luminous green digits. Still it functioned, recording and depositing neuro-chemical activity within its database, operating in synchronicity. Then, it deactivated. Although inoperative, it continued to oscillate with lateral motion.

With a shaky hand he wiped his gaunt face, which was drenched in hot sticky sweat. His eyes were dark with exhaustion. He took a deep breath fighting to take in the thin weak air and then exhaled in convulsive relief.

On his left arm he noticed a syringe inserted into his bicep. Connected to it, was a long, dangling tube which trailed off towards yet another machine. A yellowish fluid passed through the tube... a complex food source. Vigorously he pulled at it until it loosened, tossing it away. As the syringe hit the floor it cracked open, the yellowish fluid leaking out. Slowly, the fluid began to solidify and transform into a dense gooey substance as it met with the atmosphere.

Gazing around, he noticed a corroded metallic door. Struggling to his feet, he began to make his way to the exit. The muscle wastage made every step painful. For the first time he realised that he was in some kind of spherical shaped chamber. Barely maintaining his balance, he staggered to the door pushing it apprehensively. It swung open with a creak. Instantly, powerful blinding sunlight struck him. He instinctively raised his hands in an attempt to shield his eyes from the sun. Warily he stepped out and gazed towards the horizon, barely distinguishing the other chambers in the distance. They were glowing, shining silver and metallic in the alien light.

Sebastian Eckardt stood there motionless, with no recollection of his past, his mind void and empty, the memory of his trip now fading away into a meaningless blur. Dust swirled around him blown by a gust of wind, his eyes reflecting the huge shimmering orb of the sun. Ahead the land stretched for miles without moisture of any kind. An endless arid wilderness of scorching sun and broken rock engulfed him. Death was certain. He stood at its mercy, at the mercy of the unforgiving world... Citon!

Spy Hunter

The blade-roller halted beside the waiting line at the business end of level 4. Reece stepped towards it, holding out his card, jumping the queue of five waiting passengers who eyed him angrily. The passenger door opened.

"Spy Hunter, hey...? Where to?" the cab driver asked cordially.

Reece slid in, leaning back, relaxed.

"Level 1, please."

The driver inclined his head in a mark of esteem.

"Don't get too many Hunters nowadays."

The blade-roller began to move, disappearing through the endless underground network of tubular metallic passages.

Reece felt his eyes grow heavy, lulled by the motion of the blade-roller and to snap himself out of it, he reached into his pocket and pulled out the notepad and stylus he had purchased earlier. Every time he went out on a mission he seemed to feel his mortality more and more. He had decided to start keeping a journal. Maybe, one day, hopefully a day on the surface of the planet instead of deep underground where mankind had been forced to seek refuge, his descendants would find value in his words. Chewing the end of the stylus gently he wondered how to begin. Then he started writing…

Stretching across the continent of America, there was a subterranean human existence. The remainder of the planet was lifeless. Only a selected few ventured to the surface, specially licensed killers known as Spy Hunters. After the war, three centuries back, Earth was left in ruin. Hard radiation had caused mutations at all levels. Only a few tribal mutants roamed the surface of the planet in search of food, fighting for survival amongst the death and destruction. But unknown alien creatures would occasionally come from other worlds and stalk the surface with deadly intentions...

Working its way up through the various levels, the roller halted smoothly at L1. The footpath was bare, no sound or motion. Overhead, an oxygen system droned, powerful jets blasting out cold re-purified air.

"Always empty up here. Boring if you ask me..."

Reece smiled in acknowledgement, his dark brown eyes full of expression.

"What do I owe?"

"Twenty please."

He stuffed the journal and stylus back in his pocket and stretched out his hand laying it against the credit collector. Briskly it registered and bleeped. A white glow of light seeped through his fingers and around the edges of his hand.

"Credit stored," a recorded female voice chimed softly.

The door slid open.

"Must be a fascinating occupation," the driver said half grinning with admiration. "Tell me, what's it like on the surface?"

Reece halted, one foot outside on the firm ground.

"Dead, silent, radioactive... At dawn a burning sun, at nightfall a cold moon lighting the evening sky."

The driver interjected.

"I hope I live long enough to see it, to see the rhythm of the day and night, even one small miserable glance. Do you think we will ever reclaim the surface, revive earth again? I mean grow food in the ground as our ancestors did?"

"Maybe one day. Thanks for the ride."

He stepped out and the blade-roller began to move, disappearing down the tube, southbound, towards the commercial centre. Reece raised his jacket collar and commenced his walk towards the GDS assembly point, a short distance off. Consulting his wristwatch, he realised twenty minutes remained before his meeting with Lawrence Parker, head of the Government Defence system; another mission, another deadly assignment. Moments later he was there. Outside, illuminated by glowing lights, were the words 'Defenders of the Planet.'

Waving his hand in front of the code beam, he pushed through the heavy revolving doors, and entered.

"Hi Reece," the secretary said in her usual flirtatious fashion, her eyes crystal green, her aging body well preserved by hormones and specialised rejuvenation processes. He shot her a warm glance, immediately disengaging his focus as he walked into the meeting room. As always, the room was meticulously arranged, rows of chairs and desks systematically positioned. A large monitor screen hung against the wall, seemingly in suspension.

"Hey," Casper grumbled, from halfway across the room, lowering his paper, his nails cracked and broken, his face lined with fatigue, short blond hair wet and spiked. "On time..."

Reece was momentarily startled. He moved over, dropping into the chair beside him.

"I didn't see you... caught me off guard..."

"Sorry, buddy. Did you hear?" His voice became hard, serious. "It's just the two of us."

"I knew it... office gossip, never accurate. I was told it was three, me you and Wilson."

"Not anymore Reece. Why they keep cutting numbers for such dangerous missions is beyond me! Anything to save a few credits..."

Reece leaned back listening, cool and composed, a vital characteristic in such a deadly nerve-wracking job.

"I guess they can't help picking the best, strategic reasons." He winked and smiled, nudging him with a sharp elbow.

Suddenly Lawrence Parker walked in, shutting the door behind him. He was a short stocky man, partially bald with bowed legs, his gold-coloured uniform glinting in the light. He smiled across at them thinly, an unlit cigar jammed in his mouth.

"Good day gentlemen."

"How's it going Parker?" Reece inquired.

"That depends."

Parker regulated the lights from a remote control, dimming the room into virtual darkness. He then pressed a button on the remote and the large monitor screen lit up; a white, blank shimmering square of light. Parker walked over and halted beside the screen, Reece and Casper focused on him, alert and attentive.

"Let's make this short and get down to business."

He paused, lighting his cigar. At last he spoke.

"We have brief footage of four alien's stalking the surface. They are close by. Please note there could be more!"

There was an interval of silence as he puffed away, the cigar glowing red.

"Alien invaders!" Reece snapped.

"Yes. We have many enemies scattered throughout the galaxy and beyond. But I don't recognize these."

"Do you think they can replicate?"

"Replicate… methods of replication. Most certainly."

Casper gazed over at Reece apprehensively, eyes widening. Parker continued.

"We need to move fast, it's vital. As I said they are close by, roaming the surface of our planet. No time to waste! It's already been two days since the alarm! I would hate to think what would happen down here if they gained access. I'm sure they have sinister intentions! Why else would they bother to come here?"

"They could be R-Bomb carriers, kamikazes," Casper rasped worriedly.

"Yes, they could be. Most of our enemies throughout the galaxy would love to wipe us out completely and destroy this subterranean existence of ours. A massive explosion would be the easiest way to wipe us all out. Yes, these aliens could be carrying R-Bombs inside their bodies, so that they are undetectable to the eye. If they were to gain access to our underground world the consequences would be devastating. That type of bomb sets off a series of deadly controlled explosions which move for miles. Thus both of you will need to be careful, extra cautious with your approach. Get on the surface and wipe them out as soon as possible using your ray guns. Take a look at these images we captured."

Parker pointed at the screen. He pressed a button on the remote control and the blank, shimmering square of light across the screen, faded. Images began to appear. All three men looked on... The cold moon was visible through the swirling mists, the jagged mountains fading into the darkness and night vapours. He sped up the images into a blur of energy. Seconds later he slowed it down. Four aliens came into view moving in swift, jerky strides, lurking in the shadows. He pressed pause on the remote, freezing the image so that they could all take a good look. He then magnified it. There was no question the aliens were ugly. They were green and hairless. They had two legs, two arms, hands, feet, slender frames, except that their skulls were elongated, with big slanting multi-lensed eyes, a tiny slit for a mouth and no visible nose or ears.

"Boy, they are the stuff of nightmares," Casper said sharply in revulsion, tapping his mechanical pencil against his lip repetitively. "They must have vascular and pulmonary systems of some type."

In the darkness of the room Parker shut down the monitor. Then using the remote he restored light to the room. Reece blinked, readjusting to the glare.

"So men, report here tomorrow at 8am. I'm aiming to get you both out on the surface by 10am."

Back at his apartment Reece sat, ice-chilled vodka in hand. In the corner the tele-set was live and active, faintly audible; the sole news channel playing. After a time of reflection, he had finally pieced together and absorbed all the information from his meeting with Parker. '*Some more aliens to wipe out!*' he thought.

From the adjoining kitchenette, Antoinette walked over, passing from a zone of bright light into the recessed lighting of the living room. She sat beside him, arranging herself gracefully, her silk robe falling across the floor, hazel eyes warm and immense. Around her neck, a chain of colourful gems rested. He shifted his gaze towards her.

"Reece, are you ok?

"Yeah babe." he replied unconvincingly.

"Don't you think it's about time you took a break? You deserve a well-earned rest."

"Maybe one of these days..."

Her expression became serious.

"I know it pays well... but I wish you'd find another post within the GDS. Seventeen years is a long time. It's not like you are the only one. They've got up to forty registered Hunters."

She broke off, almost inviting him to agree and then tried again.

"I mean an enormous corporation like this."

"Antoinette, by law a Spy Hunter retires at 45, it's mandatory. That gives me another ten years before I can even contemplate a managerial post."

She stroked his face, her eyes full of concern.

He knocked back his drink, an ice cube falling into his mouth and melting promptly into liquid, knowing he was hurting her but unable to do anything about it.

"How long will you be gone for?"

He chose his words carefully; the risk factor was high.

"Can't say. It may prove to be a long tedious process, but hopefully not."

She pressed her hand against his chest.

"Please be careful."

"I will... as long as I have you to come back to, I always will."

From his pocket he yanked out the ticket he had purchased after the meeting.

"Here," he said holding onto her arm gently, his tender grip affirming his love and concern.

"What's this?"

"A ticket to sector 1."

She pondered for a time, visibly surprised.

"That's below the old state of California."

"Correct. The blade-roller will get you there within four hours."

"But why?"

"Sector 4 has been under constant attack as you know. Luckily, so far all has been well. However, whilst I'm away I want you out of here, somewhere safer. It's getting dangerous Antoinette. Especially now that we have detected these four aliens on the surface. They're nearby, and there could be more. They could be R-Bomb kamikaze carriers. If they get under, into Sector 4, our sector," he paused… eyes cold and distant. "The consequences could be devastating."

"Okay," she said, resigned to the fact, the same classical resignation he had seen countless times before.

"I'll go pack a bag, get some bits together. But if everyone in Sector 4 took the same approach there would be no one left here. All the other Sectors would be flooded with an overload of worried people from Sector 4."

"Please Antoinette! It's one less thing for me to worry about."

She kissed him on the lips softly and they embraced.

The next morning Reece and Casper sat in the launching chamber. Above was the exit, two thick metallic doors which separated the underground world from the surface. Gazing up Reece could sense the desolation, the remoteness that awaited them and with it the danger. Dressed in their atmospheric suits, their masks were secure, protecting them against the eye damaging sunlight that awaited them. Automatically, the mask-filtering-system activated; a refined mechanism that blocked out the hazardous airborne particles that hovered above Terra, allowing in clean oxygen. Attached to their belts were ray guns, scanners, and small tracking devices that detected distant energy fields. Reece raised his thumb.

"Let's do it."

From the mask-fitted transmitter, he gave the command.

"Duke... we're all set..."

"Did you take the nutrition-hydro capsule? You may well be out there for several days."

"Yes."

"Okay, keep us informed of your progress and good luck."

"Thanks."

The echoes of his last words faded with a series of crackles, as the transmitter deactivated. The metal ground beneath them began to move with a hum, lifting steadily, elevating a platform towards the now parting metallic doors. Sunlight and a blue sky soon became visible, light seeping through with an alien-like effect. A cold shiver rushed through Reece, suppressed by a rigid determination to see out the task. As they reached the surface they moved onto the arid ground. It resembled a wilderness, hot and dry, desolation and silence everywhere, but for the faint cries of hovering birds that came and went every now and then.

Far off, jagged mountains were visible, vivid, framed in the brilliant light. A lizard like creature suddenly moved across the ground in search of refuge. It disappeared amongst piles of brick and steel, the remains of a city; hard tall structures that once stood gracing the land, relics of the past. The platform began to descend, the doors shutting simultaneously.

"Welcome to Sunny Nevada. The diurnal nocturnal circle again," Casper muttered.

Manipulating his tracking device, Reece detected the presence of life, stretching over three miles to the north.

"Casper look!" He squeezed his arm. "Cephalic activity."

Across the luminous screen, a red light pulsed in varied sections of the map showing areas of movement, a detailed network of green lines and squares.

"It could be mutant colonies. They're scattered all over. The furthest point of activity is 3.2 miles away. After that nothing."

"Yeah, well I guess we should make headway," Casper replied, his eyes cold and bright with anticipation.

"The good thing is the device has picked up energy fields around the same congregated area. Just one straight path north. It's easy enough."

Reece pointed back at the screen, towards a section that displayed climatic data.

"The planet seems to be cooling off, who knows what the future brings. Perhaps the surface can be reclaimed one day."

As they trudged over the rugged landscape, the poisonous wind lashed around them, twisting across the ruined surface of Earth, its sound a roar reminiscent of a past existence. Heaps of rubble and remnants of civilization lay scattered across the barren hostile land, rotting, rusting; metal bent and twisted. Lifeless trees swayed back and forth, sapped dry of their moisture, shrivelling in the heat. Above, the sun shone like a blinding orb of fire; there was no escape from its clutches.

Occasionally they passed the odd mutant community; tiny huts made from timber and scrap metal; tribe after tribe of small silent communities that gazed over at them in awe, like lost children in search of guidance... of hope. Groups sat around like primitives, huddled together in rags and animal skins, conversing, jesting, others cleaning weapons, knives, arms rising and falling, gesticulating, chattering murmurs of voices drifting back and forth, an inconceivable spectacle of barbaric existence. Most were short but well built. The whites of their eyes appeared to shine, contrasting against their black leathery skin that was dirt stained and ravaged with hot burning sweat and fatigue.

"Damn mutant freaks!" Casper snapped irritably. "It's as if they are at another evolutionary stage... a bit like Neanderthal man. It's amazing how their bodies have adapted to withstand such a hostile atmosphere and terrain, toxic winds, air...good survival instincts I guess."

Reece nodded in agreement and replied, "They're certainly not sterile that's for sure. They've increased in number. It's the most I've seen at any one time. But don't forget they are Homo-Sapiens just like us. Perhaps to them we are the mutants."

"Come on, look at them. They're hideous."

Reece felt his colleague was being a little harsh.

"The war, the hydrogen explosions thinned the atmosphere, don't forget. The sun is unforgiving, merciless. I guess that's why there's such a startling contrast. Under the surface there is no ultraviolet light to raise the pigment level, nothing to burn the skin... react with the melanin, that's why subterranean humanity has evolved differently and consequently lost skin colour. It's an environmental issue, food intake and so forth, nothing more. It doesn't make this gene-damaged society inferior."

Casper did not answer his thoughts and attention straying to his tracking device... "Just one more section of red. A mile to go... Once we've passed those ruins, we'll be close. Let's keep going. Momentum at a time like this is vital."

Reece gave the thumbs up, and they moved on, disappearing between the ruins at increasing pace. Within a short time they were a hundred metres away from their target. Ahead they could see a huge spaceship. It lay across the hostile bleak ground at a tilt, unbalanced by the uneven, rocky landscape. It was silver and smooth, nothing complex looking, spherical in shape.

Reece moved forward concealing himself behind a huge rock, Casper nearby. Beneath them lay dead wispy strands of dry yellowish green grass.

"Okay, that's got to be them." hissed Reece.

Casper squatted, to break the gravity effect and alleviate the built-up strain on his legs. Reece knew that an oppressive fatigue had set in, almost draining, immobilising Casper's body. He felt it too. Casper gazed at the ship with intense curiosity, concealed from view in the dark shadow of the rock. He said, "It doesn't resemble any we've seen before. A first-class ship."

Reece slid out his bulging ray gun clicking it into action. Abruptly the ship came to life. Hatches dropped open. Moments passed, seconds. One of the alien's suddenly emerged followed by another. The enemy had finally manifested itself, captured in the periphery of their vision. Reece could vaguely detect some kind of dialogue. It was muffled, indistinct, an alien tongue.

"That's them alright."

"Yeah," Casper rasped in disgust.

Reece began to study them closely and said, "Look at them, the extended larger frontal area of the skull indicates a highly intelligent systematic brain... highly developed cognitive faculties, greater conceptual capacity."

"And?"

"Well we're going to have to exercise caution. Such a super intelligent brain could cause us a lot of trouble.

"So what's the plan Reece?"

"Plan?"

A faint smile flitted across Casper's masked features. He shook his head, gazing off into the distance. "This isn't the best moment for jokes, Reece. We need an organized strategy."

Slowly the two aliens re-entered the ship. Silence resumed. A venomous wind blew around them but soon died away.

"Let's move in Casper. We'll take it as it comes. It won't be long before they are alerted to our presence."

Rapidly, crouching, they moved towards the ship, maintaining equilibrium across the uneven ground, ray guns in hand, balanced expertly. The ship now took on another form, transforming itself from a spherical shape to a squarer one, its alloys appearing to melt, twisting and expanding as if the frame of the ship had been subjected to sudden tremendous heat. Once solidified, it began to glow faintly. An invisible energy field had been activated around it. They could almost trace it in the air, as if they had inner sensors capable of detecting changes in frequency. They paused a few meters away.

"Amazing..."

"Yeah," Casper replied in startled apprehension, eyes wide and curious.

"Look Casper, an open hatch."

"Wait," he muttered, halting Reece in his tracks. "Perhaps it's a trap."

"We'll chance it."

They entered a long ominous passageway that snaked away ahead of them. It was narrow and cold, dim floor lights leading the way down into the interior of the ship. Slowly they advanced, cautious and alert, until they reached a door shutting off the passage. Reece pointed indicating the door. Halting, they listened, acutely conscious of the light that shone through a thin aperture above and below. Casper slid to the floor, peering underneath.

"Nothing," he whispered looking up. "Can't see anything at all." He returned to his feet, looking at Reece indecisively.

There was a long, agonized pause. Reece remained silent, weighing up the situation. Then, with awareness heightened by adrenalin, he sensed the presence of life behind the door.

"Casper. Get ready," he hissed.

Reece suddenly slid the door open, charging in. Standing before him were the four aliens. Rapidly he took aim, zeroing in on them.

"Freeze... Get back."

The aliens responded by moving into a huddle, clicking, and squeaking, their multi-lensed eyes staring fiercely. Casper rushed over, waving his ray gun with both hands.

"Who sent you?" Reece demanded. "Speak!"

The aliens were terrified, uttering meaningless sounds.

"It's futile Reece, they can't speak. So what do you think? R-Bomb carriers?"

"Perhaps... I'll use the scanner."

Reece's hand flew to his belt activating the scanner. It buzzed, outcome negative.

"It registered clean."

"Good. So what next?

There was no reply. Instead Reece began looking around the chamber, studying the baffling mass of machinery that surrounded him. Lights pulsed and flashed; hums and bleeps sounding at regular intervals. In the centre stood a narrow metal rod, a device, vertically orientated, almost to the same height as the humans themselves. Suddenly, one of the aliens reached for a long thin weapon. Instinctively Reece fired, targeting the cerebral region, blasting the alien to the floor, blue and white sparks of rippling light penetrating it. He inched nearer, studying it at closer range, cradling his gun apprehensively.

"Contact base... Let them know we've tracked them down."

Casper lowered his gun by degrees, snapping on the vid-phone across his wrist. It hummed and sparked into life, flashing light against his mask. On the screen Duke's features were sharp and distinctive, even the scar on his lip that marred his face.

"We've got them. One dead already. Three to go... So far operation running smoothly... No complications."

"Present location?"

"3.2 miles from launch! On board an immobilized alien ship. These aliens had a sinister plan alright."

"Any R-Bombs found?"

"Not yet Duke, the aliens are clean, they are not carrying them internally," he said. "Reece used the scanner. They are completely clean. But they could have the R-Bombs stored somewhere on the ship." His eyes roamed.

"Okay, registered! Current position stored. All clear..."

Duke broke the connection. The image dimmed, vanishing moments later. There was silence for a time. Pulses raced. Reece was occupied in deep thought. The conduits of his brain calculating their next step.

"Casper, I'll have to inspect the ship. Let me see what I can find. There is nothing in here. I guess it's the control-room. Who knows, I might find some R-Bombs."

"Is that advisable?"

"It's a must."

"Don't stray too far," Casper cautioned. "There could be a whole army of these things."

"Yes, there could be. Who knows how many there really are? But don't worry, I'll be okay."

Reece walked over towards the corner of the chamber where another door stood, outlined in a golden rust colour. Under the pressure of his fingertips, it slid open, disappearing into the wall. Ahead lay a passageway, dots of blue light marking the way down. Slowly he advanced, heavy boots echoing against the hard floor. He raised his gun above his shoulder and continued to move ahead with caution.

He grew breathless, hesitating. Visions of what could lie ahead flashed through his mind. Nervous sweat broke out across his face. Reaching the bottom he could progress no further; a door sealed off the passageway.

Bringing his ray-gun into position, he fired, its rays eating away at the hard metallic alloys, burning a neat hole through the door. The circular piece of smoking metal fell into the chamber ahead. Reece entered, waving his gun. No sound or movement. From the silvered ceiling, beams of light shone onto the floor; a translucent light that radiated with brilliance. It seemed to him that its motion almost formed a pattern. Moving with care and trepidation, he passed through it as there was no way of avoiding it. Instantly his figure began to dim, wavering, fading until he was almost invisible, a glimmering shape of vague existence. Then, at last, he was through to the other side.

He turned his attention to the long chamber in which he found himself. It was filled with electronic and mechanical components, nothing but gadgets, wires, and circuit boards spread out across a series of circular tables. To his left, he noticed a large container. He walked over and stood gazing into a swirling vat of bubbling liquid. It appeared they were planning to construct or develop something. Reece wondered, theorising. He heard a sound. A vibration. Then silence. Although no one was in sight, he remained alert. He could almost sense the presence of others, an inner jolt; a subconscious intuition that warned him of danger.

Then, from a concealed sliding door two aliens appeared, armed with long thin weapons, just as if they had materialized from out of nowhere. Before he knew it a red destruct beam flashed past him, missing narrowly, zapping against the wall of the chamber with a metallic clang. Then another zoomed past, inches from his head. Deftly, he twisted his body and rolled across the floor. Now kneeling, he took rapid aim and fired repeatedly. The rays hit their targets, penetrating deeply. Both aliens staggered for a moment, until at last they fell onto the floor, motionless. Reece's heart thumped heavily. He lowered his ray gun and gradually regained equilibrium.

Standing up, he refocused, and began scanning the chamber, rummaging through the pile of mechanical components, hunting cautiously, finding nothing, at least nothing of any immediate relevance. He paused wondering, then hurried back towards the control-room. Running in he found it empty; Casper was gone, along with the three aliens. Even the body of the one he had shot. Immediately, a great oppression came over him, a sense of doom. Hastily, Reece consulted his vid-phone, but failed to connect.

"Casper," he yelled the rising pitch in his voice suppressed by the mask.

Waiting anxiously for a reply, doubts flooded his mind. There was nothing, only the sound of working machinery. Rapidly he headed for the exit, towards the hatch, where the growing light of day revived him with hope.

"Casper... Casper!"

The echoes of his desperate cries returned to him but there were no answers. Through the hatch he could see the desolate expanse, mountains, dust, and blinding sunlight. Again he attempted to work his vid-phone but it was totally inoperative.

The ship suddenly roared into life, rumbling with power; the floor chugged under him. The hatch door began to close. He had seconds. He had to think and act fast. Caught in the grip of conflicting emotions he rushed for the exit, leaping out. With a hard thump, he fell, colliding awkwardly with the ground. A cloud of arid dust engulfed him obscuring his vision. He waved it away, barely conscious. The roar was intense, its deafening noise causing him to regain awareness. Reece, now more alert, crawled away and lay at a safe distance.

The ground beneath began to shake. Jets roared as they burst into activity. The immense ship rose, gaining altitude, a great rushing sound filling the air. As it soared high into the atmosphere, Reece tracked its movement, eyes fixed upon it, but in a blink, it had disappeared, gone, heading out for deep space. Silence fell. A silence so abrupt it was startling. On the ground and in a daze, Reece attempted to contact base, but he began to drift into a state of unconscious.

It was night when he groggily became aware of the world around him again. Above, the moon lit the surface of Earth, cutting into the gloom. Stars stretched across the sky, infinite and tiny energetic dots of white. He closed his eyes again and slept for a while. There was a bleep, followed by another. Reece's vid-phone flashed into life. The sound roused him, breaking his solitude. His eyes opened, adjusting to the darkness.

"Reece, this is Duke. Do you copy? I repeat do you copy?"

The voice came to him as if from a great distance. Still dazed, he moved his hand wearily, gazing blankly at the brightly illuminated vid-phone with blurred vision.

"Yes, I copy," he murmured. His voice slurred low and strained.

"Are you hurt?"

"No, I'm okay, but I was out cold for a time."

He shook his head. The screen fuzzed then cleared.

"We've been trying to contact you for hours. We almost gave up hope. Give me your precise location and we'll get a rescue team out there immediately. Casper told us he searched for miles but couldn't find you."

"What?" The pitch of his voice rose. His mind began to clear, slowly restoring his thoughts and faculties into a process of normality. "You've heard from him?"

"He's with us, alive and well. He's at the medical centre undergoing the standard routine tests for after-surface exposure."

Reece stood up, regaining strength, his dizziness fading. His initial pleasure at hearing his friend was safe suddenly gave way to a nagging doubt.

"But... but I don't understand, that's not possible. He was taken up in the ship. At least that's how it seemed."

"He got away. He re-entered two hours ago."

Reece was puzzled, trying to make sense of it all. It just didn't seem to add up. He thought back, frowning, frantically switching from scene to scene in his mind, looking into one possibility after another. '*The ship, the aliens... the room full of wires, gadgets, circuit boards and mechanical components. What were they building?*

Perhaps a machine...?' He pondered further, deeper. *'A robot...! An R-Bomb carrier! Perhaps... perhaps...?'*

"Duke, listen you've got to..."

Before he could complete his sentence the vid-phone suddenly cut out, all sound, images, and light with it. The blackness of night returned, and the ground beneath him shook violently. His mouth opened in a soundless scream, his eyes staring in blind horror.

Out in space, in the ship, an alien sat in the control room manipulating buttons and levers idly. It then dialled a series of numbers across the control module, raising the communication cone to its mouth.

"Commander, Mission accomplished. The R-Bomb robot carrier which replaced the human was perfect, constructed with high precision accuracy, identical to the human hostage. The R-bomb was set to explode at the trigger phase."

"Great. How long before it detonates?"

The alien turned a dial, gazing at the screen.

"It has Commander. It already has."

Mind Blitz

THEY moved like ants, powerful and metallic. Robots were everywhere. Planet E, the new Earth was totally governed by machine, along with all the other earth colonies within the solar-system and beyond. They had defeated the humans in a long bitter war which had now ended. Special signals were emitted from the central governing base scanning the minds of man, all cephalic activity, electrical and chemical, thus giving robots complete control. All thoughts were continuously extracted, analyzed then the complete gestalt, the ultimate robot mind invasion. The heterogeneous world had ended, the homogeneous had begun. Even dreams were recorded. The advertisement boards around the planet read, 'Pure thoughts only, Negative thoughts can be punishable by death.'

Detective Elio Decker, a robot, had just flown in from Mars. Making its way out of the spaceport, it caught a hover-cab. The cab ascended into the atmosphere at a steady velocity, the City of New York slowly fading away. Achieving the correct altitude, it glided horizontally, the driver allowing the autonomic circuit to make the journey. Elio gazed mechanically into the evening twilight. In the distance, it registered ships heading for outer space; tiny metallic glints lost in the red tinted sky.

Suddenly, the intercom attached to its steel wrist buzzed.

"We still haven't found him."

"Keep searching. I want him found soon."

The next day, a team of robot police beat down the door of an apartment on Wickers Street, New York.

"Jefferson Santa Cruz," an officer yelled rushing in, its voice harsh and guttural. It clutched its long thin beam-rifle, pointing it, staring into a vacant room, other officers swarming behind.

"He's gotten away again."

The Chief Inspector walked over.

"He can't be too far. Can you smell him?" it rasped with metallic revulsion, its mechanical eyes roaming, searching. The officer nodded with distaste. The human scent was still acutely present, bedcovers spread and creased. A can of shaving foam lay on the warm metal floor, a streak of foam seeping from it. Clothes were tossed across the bathroom sink in a knot of confusion, a gold chain lying across it sparkling in the light. Feverishly, the team of robot police began inspecting, turning the room upside down.

Down the street, concealed amongst a small crowd of noisy school kids, Jefferson darted towards a red vehicle, sunlight dazzling his eyes, snow everywhere. The cold roused him, clouds of vapour puffing from his mouth.

"Hurry, get in, quick," Athena cried, waving her heavily jewelled hand. The door opened automatically. He threw himself into a seat, slamming the door behind him with force.

"They just busted in! A whole team of those stinking machines! I caught a glimpse. They were everywhere."

The air-car moved with power, ascending into the sky steadily.

"Stay calm," he said regaining his breath, his neck and white shirt damp with sweat. "Do you have it on? They can track us otherwise and scan your brain."

She moved her hair away from her face and with a finger lifted her earlobe, clearly exposing the tiny black clipped device; a signal breaker which he had designed and made.

"Of course I have it on. You are always panicking. For the last five years this has become a part of my anatomy. It's constantly clipped to my earlobe."

"Good. Sorry, I get a little paranoid at times."

"Don't worry. It's okay," she replied softly. "Even five years on, it's still amazing to think that this small contraption allows my thoughts and ideas to remain mine, solely mine, and that they are not displayed in that damn control centre for robot consumption. I still can't believe how most of the population just accept it."

He wiped his neck with a hanky soaking perspiration and replied.

"As I have told you countless times before, ever since the mind blitz started, human beings have been completely brainwashed Athena. Slow progressive mind manipulation. The robots play on the notion of pure thinking. To rebel means to have evil intentions, ideas... evil thoughts. The general public have embraced it religiously; at least for now. In time things may change."

They landed in a field five miles outside the city centre, heavy tires marring the hard packed snow, dead trees frozen with winter chill.

"Where are we heading exactly?" asked Jefferson.

"The family cottage I call it. You have never been there before."

"How long will it take to get there?"

"It's only a few miles from here."

"Okay." He turned scanning the landscape; his mind deeply entrenched in thought.

At the cottage beside a blazing synthetic fire, Jefferson warmed his hands, his eyes bright in the firelight. The room itself contained nothing but a light grey sofa. Sections were torn and stained. The surrounding timber walls were dusty, cracked with age and neglect. The cottage location was ideal, locked away from the endless tide of noise and manic city life. No sound, no motion, nothing but snow-covered nature engulfing them in all directions.

"How long have you had this place?"

"Years. It's been passed down through the generations. It originally belonged to my great grandfather. I spent many years living here as a child with my parents."

He smiled. "I see. In all the years I've known you, I never knew you had this place."

"Yes, I know. Ever since my parents died this place has been left semi-abandoned. But rather than taking you back to my apartment as I usually do, I thought I would take you here this time. It feels a little safer."

Her expression now became serious, urgent.

"Anyway Jefferson, what are we to do? They're going to get us sooner or later, especially with all their special technology. They'll cover mile after mile of land until they reach us. We are hanging onto borrowed time."

"Maybe." His voice suddenly rose. "If only we could get a ship out of here."

"Where too?"

"Preferably out of this solar system. There are a few remaining planets and moons in our galaxy that remain under the old law of free thinking, several in fact. If only we could get to one of those. Having said that, Jupiter's moon Ganymede is the only one in this solar system that is free from the mind blitz, so that too is a possible option for us and it's the closest one to us. Of course we would have to take off from Asia. It's the only continent that journeys to these planets and moons... ones that are free from the mind-blitz. Getting to Asia is a major problem. It's so far. Not to mention that even if we got there, robot police at the spaceports would be waiting for us. We wouldn't even get through customs. We would be arrested on the spot."

"Yes, true... But these few remaining planets and moons in our galaxy including Ganymede are all still under Robot control anyway."

"Yes, unfortunately we can't escape that, Athena. Machines now control everything but at least they are all free from the mind blitz. All the humans that dwell on these planets and moons are free, free from mind-control, thus they remain human."

He began pacing up and down the room in angered contemplation, bitter and dispirited. Tree branches slapped against the window, powered by the wind.

"Another option is to fight the machines and destroy them, but we will need great numbers. I have correlated all the facts. Statistically most humans accept the mind blitz but there are growing numbers who want out. If only we could reach these segregated groups and individuals before the robot police agents do, we could potentially build an army. But it won't be easy."

He paused. His cold grey eyes dilated.

"There are many that want to be human again."

Athena shot him a confused look.

"Human?"

"Yes Athena. Human means to have independent thought and for it to remain within the confines of the individual's mind. Aside from us, at present, all living humans here on Earth are mind-controlled, completely enslaved. In fact, aside from those planets and moons, including Ganymede, all human beings throughout the galaxy are mind controlled. They have become like cattle. Denuded, stripped of their will to be. Their free will has been taken away from them. Free will, the ability to act and think privately for oneself is what makes us human. Once you take that away from people, they become dehumanized, like an organic robot. The science behind scanning people's brains is this…Hacking into the human brain requires decoding the logic of neurons. The brain is a complex network of approximately one hundred billion neurons. Different experiences create different neural connections which bring about different emotions and so forth. As you know they can even record dreams via a dream recording machine. This device uses advanced technology to capture the complex activity in a human brain when we dream. It then turns this activity into images and videos that can be observed. It uses functional magnetic resonance imaging to measure brain activity and figure out what a human being is dreaming about. Then special computer programs help turn this information into pictures and videos representing dreams. Furthermore, using a modified MRI machine, these robots were able to identify specific brain activity patterns occurring while people dreamed about different scenarios. The MRI scanner then analyses the patterns through computer algorithms, creating images that represent the 'visuals' one experiences during dreams. Their findings revealed that our brains respond similarly to visual stimuli whether we are awake or asleep. This means that it is possible to decode dreams using functional magnetic resonance imaging (MRI) machines which detect changes in blood flow within the brain. The device then harnesses the power of deep learning and neural networks to bridge the gap between the subjective experience of dreams and objective visual representation."

He walked over to the sofa and sat; arms folded. Then, there was a sudden roar. The cottage windows vibrated faintly, bits of hard accumulated ice breaking off and falling to the ground below. Jefferson darted to the window. He could see a patrol-air-car landing, green descent lights winking on and off, almost lost in the sparkling morning sunlight.

"Robot cops! Quick, let's move…"

Her eyes widened, her face turning chalk white with cold fear. Abruptly they turned and fled. Outside a team of four robots rushed towards the front door.

"Santa Cruz, open up! You have three seconds," one rasped sharply, its voice seeking to penetrate the thickness of the door. After an interval of silence, they opened fire with a series of blasts from their beam-rifles and the door was consumed into nothingness. All that remained was a hovering cloud of greyish dust particles. A window cracked from the sudden pressure, a fine web of hair line fractures splintering in all directions. They moved in fast, mechanically, scanning and probing. The wood beneath them creaked and split, giving way to the immense metallic weight that besieged it.

At the back of the cottage, Jefferson and Athena darted out from an escape door, rushing furiously towards the forest, pushing branches out of the way in panic. As they moved deeper into the endless forest of silent towering trees, the wind battered against them, almost halting them in their tracks. Even the elements appeared to conspire against them. Finally they stopped, regaining breath in the chill winter air, staring, listening. Above, a flock of birds fluttered away breaking formation, their sound and motion unnerving.

"Jefferson," Athena croaked, her heart pounding, chest rising and falling with the effort of breathing. "What do we do now?"

Deftly, he snapped on his map-watch, fingers glued to the dials. Green lights lit, flashing dimly against his skin.

"Athena we can't go back. If we keep moving north, we'll come to a road a mile away. We're heading in the right direction for the city."

"But it's too dangerous there."

"What choice do we have?"

Suddenly, the four robot police appeared, fallen branches cracking, crunching, and splintering beneath them, sunlight sparkling across the bare metal sections of their bodies.

"Arrest them!" one yelled, its voice harsh and penetrating.

Two stormed over, one grabbing Athena, securing locks around her feet and hands. She was motionless, speechless, as if gripped by a paralysis. Her mouth gaped, lips trembling, eyes inflamed with muted urgency.

"You know your rights, don't you Sir?" the other said grabbing the signal breaker from Jefferson's earlobe and then driving a beam-rifle into his ribs. He jolted back, hands raised, the stark realization of defeat etched into his features. The robot's mechanical eyes were severe. Scanning Jefferson, it took various readings.

"We should eliminate him."

"No, we have strict orders to bring him back alive."

The robot slammed its fist into Jefferson's face with decisive impact. He staggered back and forth until he fell heavily onto the hard snow. His head spun. His ears rang. Darkness and light engulfed him fading and receding. The drifting sparks soon passed. He blinked regaining consciousness, gradual comprehension coming to him.

"Get up Santa Cruz, it's time…."

In the evening gloom, alive with sound and activity, the city of New York was glowing with light, glistening in the endless piles of white snow. Above police patrol cars circled the sky, ghostly outlines of metal in motion disappearing into the cold night. Around the Police State headquarters, a strange murky haze hovered ominously. Jefferson sat inside a room alone under bright penetrating lights in front of a bare metal table. He was rigid with apprehension. His head ached, each minute passing like a breathless hour. At the sound of approaching footsteps he swallowed weakly, hours of questioning had him in a daze. The robot police had bombarded him with many questions. But he hadn't complied, remaining silent instead. His heart began to palpitate. The door melted away. Detective Elio Decker now walked in for the first time. It sat facing Jefferson. It was now its turn to question the human subject.

"Santa Cruz we have blitzed Athena's mind completely since removing the signal breaker, however we have been unable to probe yours. Why?"

Jefferson smirked.

"Answer me!" Its voice rose as it regarded him, trying to fathom his reaction and ironically his thoughts. "Up until now you have not answered any questions. The police officers that interrogated you are very frustrated. But you will talk to me."

"What have you done with Athena?"

"She has been imprisoned, awaiting trial, basically a death sentence. Ever since the mind blitz law came into effect five years ago, you successfully devised a way to cut off the signal. Remarkable! I take it that you built the signal breakers yourself?"

"Yes of course."

"Smart. You do realise this crime is punishable by death?"

"Yes, but then again, to strip a human of his basic rights, to remove our individuality, our ability to think freely is death anyway is it not?"

"You are entitled to your opinion."

"Am I?" Jefferson replied sarcastically.

"The law is the law. Why would anyone rebel against it unless he or she is guilty of something evil, evil thoughts, evil intentions?"

"Nonsense! The privacy of the human mind should not be tampered with regardless. It is sacred. To look into people's brains, and scan their thoughts is criminal. Mankind has become nothing other than an organic robot. Human beings were created to be free in every sense of the word."

"Santa Cruz, ever since the implementation of the mind blitz, crimes have gone down from 85 percent to almost 3 percent in the New York State alone. People are forced to train their minds to think pure. When your thoughts and ideas are good, so too will be your actions."

"Everyone has bad thoughts and desires at some point, regardless. It's a part of human nature."

"Indeed, the system filters out the severe from the trivial. As a result we prevent crimes by looking into people's minds. Prevention is better than cure. The benefits are enormous. We have long files on every single human being, records of all their thoughts, aside from you and Athena."

The door melted away. A robot officer walked in. It bent beside Elio and spoke, its focus fixed towards Jefferson as if ready to pounce.

"It's no use. We've kept trying and have failed. We simply cannot read Santa Cruz's thoughts since removing his signal breaker. We have only been able to gather basic encephalic data, nothing more."

"Okay."

The robot officer turned and left the cell. Elio shut its robotic eyes, pressing its hands together. It opened them suddenly.

"Here's the deal."

Jefferson shuffled in his seat, his interest piqued, faint hope stirring inside him. Yanking out the signal breaker, Elio placed it on the table.

"Aside from this small contraption that you made," it pointed at the device keeping its eyes on him. "What other method are you using to break the signal? If you disclose this information," it held back for a second as if jostling with an idea. "You'll be a free man. I'll even free Athena. Both your lives will be spared. You have my word."

Jefferson sat up, eyes wide with surprise and confusion.

"Obviously you understand you will have to leave the planet. There is no place for a person like you in this society. You're a criminal. Your face has been seen all over the news. You are hated by your own kind. However, Athena will have to remain here on planet Earth governed by the mind blitz. As I mentioned, we have now locked into her brain since removing the signal breaker. She'll soon rejoin the mind-controlled society here on Earth once you have given me the necessary information of course."

An ice-cold feeling cut through him.

"Where will I go exactly?"

"There are several planets and moons outside our solar system in our galaxy, ones that retain the old method of free thinking, ones with soaring crimes rates and warped activity. However, if you are to remain within this solar system, your only option would be Ganymede."

"Yes, I'm aware of all this. I hope I can trust you?"

Elio stood, its powerful metallic arms crossed.

"Yes, you can trust me. You have my word but then again, what other choice do you really have? Anyway, we will soon decide where to send you exactly. The final decision will be made within the next few hours."

Jefferson bit away at his lip deep in thought.

"As I'm sure you know only too well, you would have to takeoff from Asia. It's the only continent that journeys to these planets and moons. An inter-continental cruiser will pick you up tomorrow morning. So be ready. You're in for a long, long ride... The Pacific tunnel is now open. It will drive you through the Pacific Ocean into Asia from Vancouver, Canada... Tomorrow morning we will let you know which Asian country you will depart from. Again the decision will be made within the next few hours. Well, what is your decision? Are you going to talk?"

Jefferson ran his hand through his hair. He considered for a time, weighing up his words. If he complied both Athena's and his life would be spared. He was bitterly sad that he would have to leave his good friend Athena behind. She would remain on planet Earth joining the mind-controlled society. But at least her life would be spared. He took a long deep breath...

"There's an undetectable miniature chip, a tiny chip stored in my brain which breaks the signal, and as a result synapse speed immediately increases, causing a rise in intelligence."

"Go on..."

"I built it in an underground base, alone. It then had to be surgically implanted. The man who performed the operation was an old doctor, a good friend, Leonhard Ackermann. He too wore the signal breaker to great effect. Sadly he committed suicide. He couldn't live anymore in this sick, twisted, mind-controlled society even though he wore the signal breaker and was free from the mind blitz. Anyway, he performed the operation placing the tiny chip into my brain, in the Limbic system... exact location, Hippocampus. It can't be removed. It worked with immediate effect. There is no way of undoing it."

"How did you make it?"

"I have all the scientific information right here."

"Where?"

Jefferson pulled off his map-watch, pushing it across the metal table.

"Type in the Password DELTA - 5. All the information and data will then be displayed."

Elio held it in its metallic palm.

"Have you exchanged the formula with anyone else?"

"No."

"How many of these chips have you made?"

"Just the one. Unfortunately Athena had to rely on the signal breaker alone. My deceased doctor friend too whilst he was alive."

"Tell me something. Why were you wearing the signal breaker then? I mean this chip works perfectly."

"Although I knew the chip would work perfectly, I still continued to wear the signal breaker just in case anything went wrong with the brain chip, like a sudden malfunction, even though that is extremely unlikely."

Elio slammed the buzzer across the table. Instantly a robot officer entered.

"Take this to CIP for analysis."

"Yes Detective."

Elio refocused, staring at Jefferson with cold unemotional eyes.

"You're a lucky man Santa Cruz."

"Maybe so, but you do realise others will revolt in time. As we speak there are growing numbers who want out."

"Yes indeed, and those very people are being tracked down and brought to justice. Robots control."

Jefferson snapped back.

"You can't win. You can't keep people in bondage forever. There will be a day when the citizens of this planet will fight for freedom, believe me. That day will come."

"It's our job to prevent that. We have made sure such an up-rising will not occur. You have quite an imagination Santa Cruz."

"Believe me, in time this mind invasion will come to an end. You can't control people forever."

"Jefferson Santa Cruz, you are full of dreams. Robots have created a virtually crimeless society using mind control, right or wrong, and it shall remain. Just be glad that you and Athena have had your lives spared. All that awaits you now is a distant sphere, a place far away where you belong."

Inside the confines of a cold dark cell, Jefferson lay on a bed. Across his face the moonlight shone as he gazed towards the barred window. Above, stars slid in and out of the matted layer of bitter fog. Hours had passed... hours of contemplation wondering what awaited him, what the future would bring. It would be hard living in another world. It would take time to adjust, time to adapt, but at least he would be free, free to be an individual. If only he had worked on reaching those segregated groups, the very ones that wanted out of the mind blitz, things could have been different on Earth, perhaps things would have changed. Perhaps he could have been the pioneer behind a huge revolt that would have seen the mind blitz end. All this was hypothetical now, the fact remained, it would never happen.

On the horizon a streak of amber light appeared. The sun rose steadily, and in the growing light of day the city began to take shape and form. Rising higher and through broken cloud, the sun beamed down sparkling across lawns and sidewalks, a white blinding glare flooding the streets.

Outside the Police State headquarters, mind-controlled news reporters and angry crowds circled the building suppressed by a team of robot-police forming a metallic shield. The city was alive, exploding into a torrent of sound and activity, swelling cries of indignation. Banners read: Kill the criminal Santa Cruz. Why keep him alive? Don't send him to Ganymede! Kill him! Kill him!

Inside his soundproof cell, Jefferson stood at the sink, a robotic shaving arm cutting steadily into his stubble leaving his face fresh and clean. Suddenly, a robot guard stepped into the cell accompanied by Elio.

"Are you all set?" snapped Elio sharply.

Jefferson turned slowly and replied, "Yes, I am."

"You do realise there are hundreds of angry people outside? The news has filtered through to the masses. They are all curious as to why we are keeping you alive. They all want to see you dead. You are hated by your own kind."

Silently without reply, Jefferson zipped up the blue uniform he had been provided with. He was not interested in what the mind-controlled masses thought of him. To his way of thinking, they were all lobotomised.

Elio continued... "Anyway, everything has been set up for you. All decisions made. You will be taken to Shanghai, China. You'll takeoff from there, the Shanghai City Space-Port. Robot police will be waiting for you there. As for your new home it will be Jupiter's moon Ganymede. That's the decision we have made. It's a world filled with violence and crime, no mind blitz there, total freedom of thought, the only place in this solar system like it. All the humans there live like savages as you will soon discover. Come, it's time."

As the glass elevator reached ground level, it halted with a buzz. The sound of the angry crowds was now growing louder and more ferocious as they headed for the exit. Jefferson tried to remain calm as he stepped out into the cold morning air along with Elio and the robot guard. A wall of sound struck him, stinging his ears.

"Don't send Santa Cruz to Ganymede. Kill him as he deserves. He's evil! Kill him!" A toothless old man cried pointing. Others shouted in unison, "He deserves the death penalty."

A young blonde woman then blasted icily, bracing herself in the numbing cold, a dot of red glowing across both cheeks, "A good innocent man has no reason to hide his thoughts. Kill him... he doesn't deserve to live."

A group of youths pelted stones in his direction, their eyes filled with disgust. A crew of reporters attempted to squeeze through the team of guarding police. Jefferson was gripped with fearless anger as he gazed around at the brainwashed, mind-controlled, lobotomised crowds, including the reporters. He despised them all.

Reaching the cruiser, the door automatically slid open. He stepped in and sat. The robot driver then set the powerful engine into motion. The cruiser roared almost like a lion. Elio walked over to the cruiser and halted by the open door staring at Jefferson silently. Jefferson's eyes locked with the machine. Seconds later the robot driver activated a switch and the door closed. Security bolts locked into place with a series of clicks. Inside all sound was cut off with immediate effect. The cruiser now began to move away, slowly gaining speed. Jefferson looked back. He could see hundreds of angry faces devoid of sympathy. Some pointed and shouted. Others curious...

'*What hope was there for humanity*,' he thought miserably, '*when your mind, thoughts and ideas are no longer your own?*'

Memoirs of Time

Boris Muller stood gazing at the time-sphere with immense satisfaction. It was designed with acute precision, a highly complex machine that would defy the laws of science and time.

"That's it, two years to the day and we have finally achieved our objective. This device represents a thousand years of science and mathematics."

He turned with suave authority and walked over towards Claude, hands behind his back, analysing, thinking, his hair wild and grey, bits of stubble poking from his chin.

"Can you imagine? This machine is capable of carrying a human not only into the past, but also into the future; but it's the past that interests me at present."

He smiled, confidence emanating from his eyes, his geniality and wonderfully convoluted mind clearly displayed on his countenance.

"To have found the key that unlocks the door of time is possibly the greatest achievement of man. The past, present and future is frozen in time and space. With this machine we can unlock that door and enter within and see into the future, move into the past."

"Yes Boris, but I'm still concerned. We need to look at the possible consequences, the possible dangers. It's high risk. Your presence alone could alter history, the present, and in turn, the future. You could start a never-ending time shift. A chain reaction..."

"Don't allow your thalamic impulses to take control. Existence itself is a risk. Remember, risk is the key factor in success. You need to change your mind-set. To make history, demands risk. I'm only going to briefly observe, nothing more. Observing is a minor risk. I will visit ancient China, ancient Egypt, Constantinople, the Byzantine period, and medieval England."

Boris paused then continued.

"The food, drink, and medicine that we consume each day are plagued with risk and severe collateral effects; preservatives, sweeteners and chemicals that are altering the body at a genetic level causing cancers, destabilising the balance of neurotransmitters, serotonin, dopamine, giving rise to neurological problems, depressions, psychosomatic disorders. Yet we still ignore that risk. If we are to make history, we need to be devoid of fear."

He was caught in thought, looking around his workshop, bolts and screws lying all around.

"Time travel, illegal, forbidden... Those were the words from the authorities when they had heard about our work, our project."

A few moments of silence passed.

"Claude?" Boris looked into his eyes. The doubt and anxiety were gone. He was relieved to see they were cold and hard, devoid of fear.

"It's time to put to a test this mind-blowing theorem of space-time continuum."

Claude was expecting it to happen but when the time-sphere materialised he was still startled by its sudden appearance. He drew breath, pushed back his hair, and walked over to it in awe. Lights flashed and flickered, lighting Boris's face as he sat in front of the bank of controls deactivating the machine.

"You're back! It worked!"

Boris pressed the eject button, releasing the door, with it the scent of the past. He stepped out from the cold metallic sphere. Claude's eyes lit with anticipation.

"Well, what happened?"

"I was there, back in time as incredulous as it seems. The minute I pressed the button everything went black in an incomprehensible flash, as if time had ceased for a moment. Then suddenly light, a blinding light and in that forming light, the landscape before me began to take shape and form."

Boris's face was alive with radiance in a way Claude had never seen it before. His expression said it all with muted clarity.

"I saw Ancient China, during the Shang dynasty, 1677 BC, the buildings, the landscape, and their wonderful costumes. I saw Ancient Egypt during the early period of Cleopatra's reign, 51 BC, the pyramids, the Nile, people going about their daily activities. I saw the glorious city of Constantinople, the Byzantine Empire, otherwise known as the Eastern Roman Empire, 395 AD. My last stop was medieval England, 550 AD, the Anglo-Saxons. I stood and simply observed what I could without being noticed. It's amazing to think how time has changed things, how technology and knowledge have revolutionised the world yet there is a common element that unifies man throughout history and time."

"Which is?"

"Man is still in search."

"Of...?"

"Meaning...! The very meaning of our existence... Since the dawn of man we have searched for meaning, the essence of our being, the notion of existence. The Cynics of ancient Greece grappled with the idea. Great philosophers throughout the ages thought long and hard, Socrates, Antisthenes, Plato, Aristotle but it seems we are none the closer to unravelling the puzzle, the puzzle of life."

"Purpose, the meaning of life and what lies beyond, are subjective Boris."

"Yes, but that's only personal opinion. There can be only one absolute definitive truth as to why."

Claude rubbed his jaw in thought.

"Why these sudden existential thoughts? What prompted this sudden metamorphosis?"

"I guess I've always been interested in philosophy, metaphysics, metaphysical cosmology, ontology, the universe, how it got here. It's incredible to think of all the billions of people that lived, and died, the cycle of life, an ongoing conveyer belt. What absurd purpose could man have in this infinite universe? What role does he play? What propelled life into being? We grow old and die due to the movement of time. Man struggles to remain young. Why? Aside from the obvious, it's because deep down within the subconscious of man we associate ageing with death. Hence to remain young gives man a temporal feeling of immortality and yet inevitably death awaits us all. Perhaps we live on, if so, we are immortal, eternal."

Claude stood in silence, assimilating Boris's words.

"These are not rhetorical questions Claude. They need to be answered if we are to encapsulate the meaning of our existence. I have never forgotten the final words of my grandfather. He had such a profound unifying concept of life."

Boris paused, eyes distant and reflective.

"Man is held within the sphere of time and space but beyond it lies another realm."

He Dreams Planet Earth

The giant rotating sphere that was Earth shone brilliantly. Luna's two-week period of darkness was bleak, earthlight somewhat illuminating its barren surface. The two-week diurnal cycle would soon follow, the Sun beating down mercilessly. Daylight was much brighter and harsher than the Earth's. Luna had a very, very thin atmosphere that barely scattered the light, an exosphere to be exact, and no ozone layer to repel the sun's burning ultraviolet light.

Inside his oxygen-pumped lunar home, Brent Juskowiak sat contemplating, thinking about Imperial Earth. For years he'd longed to be there and see its majestic forests and landscapes. The images burned in his mind. He pictured the Himalayas, the Atlantic Ocean, the pyramids of Egypt, the Great Wall of China but they all soon faded into an unreachable haze. Sadly, he rose from his bed and walked over to the thick glass window and gazed into the lunar darkness. His eyes caught sight of planet Earth. Suddenly his father stepped into the bedroom interrupting his imaginings.

"Brent, I've just finished my book. Three hundred pages on science, philosophy, and theology. A book like this is desperately needed on Earth."

Brent was unresponsive, his eyes fixed into the void.

"What's wrong son?"

"Dad, I would love to see Imperial Earth, even spend a day there. After all we are its descendants."

"Son, we have had this discussion before."

His dad walked over, head down. Resting his hand on his son's back he too looked out into the darkness. Up in the distance, he could see Planet Earth.

"Son, I understand how you feel, but the Moon broke away from Earth's hold for a valid reason. Since the moon's independence there has been peace. Our government here is centred on a loving theistic philosophy. Earth's government is centred on a brutal atheistic philosophy. They may control all the planets within our solar-system and beyond, but we stand alone as a jewel in space, the only theistic sphere in the galaxy. The supreme power that governs Earth and all its colonies takes its route from many different civilisations and groups throughout time, starting with the Babylonian and Egyptian mystery cults, the Kabbalistic mystery religions, the Gnostics, the Assassin cult or Ḥashshāshīn, the Knights Templar, the Jesuits and so on. The power that controls has stripped mankind of free will. They control society through mind control. They emit special signals that scan the brains of man, highly complex signals, which have the capacity to extract all cephalic data. These signals can translate brainwave patterns into words. Their excuse, mind control prevents crime; it's the ultimate crime prevention. The citizens of Earth have embraced it religiously. Son, scientifically speaking this is how it works: hacking into the human brain requires decoding the logic of neurons. Since thoughts are physical and have spatial dimensions, they can lock in and read a person's thoughts via brain wave patterns - neuronal activity. Some thoughts are consolidated as memories. Memory too is a physical process, encoded by structural molecular changes in neuronal connections... The French Philosopher Rene Descartes once said, '*Except for our own thoughts, there is nothing absolutely in our power.'* Son, if you remove freedom of thought, man becomes a machine, a robot. Remember even God gave man free will." His father paused. He rubbed his long white beard, his old eyes calm and reflective. "I think the only remaining affinity between us and them is that the Moon is in synchronous rotation with Earth, tidal locking, and that the Moon's gravitational influence produces the ocean tides. Forget Earth son."

His dad patted him on the back then walked out. Brent reflected on his words. *'Maybe one day things will change,'* he thought, *'but for now Imperial Earth remains nothing but an unapproachable planet'*.

The Edge of Eternity

He was lost in the vastness of space amongst the infinite stars. Alexis Falco had completed his two-year work assignment on the Red Planet, building the Mars-based radars which were used to discover asteroids. Powerful computers would calculate their orbits: all data and information were then stored. From the strength of the radar-echo, asteroid diameters were attained. Many asteroids were lost to the Sun, its gravitational field capturing the giant, high velocity rocks. Alone on the small ship with only the two pilots aboard, Alexis thought about the journey. He read the data screen before him. Earth and Mars were currently at their closest points, separated by a distance of 55 million kilometres.

Mars had finally gained its independence from Earth. Much tension had grown between the two planets. All people born on Mars were no longer classified as 'human' but were known as Martians despite the biological and neurological essentials that made Man remaining the same. Through the small square side window, Alexis gazed into the darkness as the ship moved fluidly through the silence of deep space.

Months passed... The roaring ship approached Earth. It plunged rapidly into its atmosphere manoeuvring for descent. The Planet glowed with splendour. The sun sparkled with brilliance; the ever-present nuclear reactor. Alexis sat up. He was almost home. Green fields slowly came into focus, the flow of life on terra. Suddenly, only meters away, the ship lost power. Betrayed by gravity, it fell like a stone and hit the hard ground beneath. The ship slid violently across the land-way. Fire raged as it came to a halt. Then silence...

Through the thick darkness of the unconscious world Alexis opened his eyes.

"Mr Falco you were very close to death."

Alexis looked up, startled. Standing before him was an old man with piercing blue eyes, casually dressed.

"Your ship crashed killing both pilots. Miraculously all you have are a few bruises and cuts but you will need to remain in hospital for a while."

Alexis sat upright. He was in a private room. He began to recollect his journey from Mars, the accident, and his final minutes of consciousness.

"I guess it wasn't my time. Who are you anyway? You don't look like a doctor?"

"Correct, I'm not a doctor, I'm a Theologian."

"Theologian...? What are you doing here with me, and how do you know my name?"

"Well as a Theologian, I often visit sick patients. You're not the first. As for your name, well the nurse who is looking after you supplied me with that information."

The Theologian inched closer to the bed.

"Mr Falco, tell me, what do you think would have happened to you had you died?"

There were a few moments of silence. A ray of sunlight filtered into the room.

"What do you mean?"

"Have you ever wondered what lies beyond?"

"At death we cease to exist."

"That's the world's view, the atheistic doctrine that sadly grips our world today. But this theory fails at so many levels; in fact it's in opposition to science. Energy cannot be destroyed. Thus, ask yourself this: at death, what happens to that invisible energy of the brain known as consciousness? The first law of thermodynamics, the conservation of energy states; energy cannot be created or destroyed but can be transformed from one form to another. The implications are vast... We are immortal from a spiritual perspective. Physics declares this irrevocably."

Alexis' still battling the daze he was in, managed to remain focused, absorbing what the man had said.

"Mr Falco, there is another dimension beyond three-dimensional space, a spiritual realm that can be defined as the ultimate reality."

Gathering his broken thoughts and trying to shake off the stupor he was still in, Alexis replied fuelled by adrenaline, "You speak with such certainty? As far as I'm concerned, no religion has relevance in today's world. In fact, science and reason has reformed man. Science and God cannot coexist. The French revolution back in 1789 was the turning point in human history... the Enlightenment, the Age of Reason, the cultural movement of intellectuals. The Enlightenment influenced the development of Atheism because it encouraged people to be sceptical."

The theologian rubbed his jaw thoughtfully, his eyes bright, and said, "Mr Falco I'm aware of all the historical facts you have just mentioned but, you know, many of the great philosophers whose work influenced the Enlightenment were actually theists, like Gottfried Leibniz, and Francis Bacon. Both men believed in God. As for the French revolution, that was initiated by the secret society known as the Illuminati headed by Adam Weishaupt. Weishaupt, as I'm sure you know was a German philosopher, a professor of civil law and later canon law. He was the founder of a group called the Illuminati; an occult group of leading thinkers that still exist to this very day. Regardless of all the history Mr Falco, God exists eternally outside of the sphere of space and time."

Moments of silence passed…

"Sir," snapped Alexis impatiently, not entirely welcoming philosophical debate right now, "before I ask you the big question, I want to share this with you, because I think it's important…. Quantum theory implies the entire Universe is preordained. In physics, determinism means that the state of the Universe at any given time and the basic laws of physics fully determine the Universe's backward history and forward evolution. This idea reached its peak with the strict, precise laws about how the Universe behaves introduced by classical physics. Take Isaac Newton's laws of motion. If someone knew the present positions and momenta of all particles, they could in theory use Newton's laws to deduce all facts about the Universe, past and future. It is only a lack of knowledge or computational power that prevents scientists from doing so. Every state of the Universe can be completely explained by an earlier one. If the Universe is a train, determinism says that it is running on a track, with no option to switch to any other path because different tracks never cross. Determinism means there is no freewill: if the laws of physics are deterministic, and our actions are just the summation of particle interactions, there seems to be no room for us to freely choose A instead of B, because the earlier states of the Universe will already have determined the outcome of our choice. And if we are not free, how can we be praised or blamed for our actions? This causes theological problems! In fact, the quantum Universe could actually be more deterministic than classical. Newton's laws allow situations in which the past does not determine how things will move in the future. For example, the laws do not provide an upper bound on how much an object can be accelerated, so in theory a classical object can reach spatial infinity in finite time. Reverse this process, and you get what have been called 'space invaders' - objects that come from spatial infinity with no causal connection to anything else in the Universe, and which cannot be predicted from any of the Universe's past states. Furthermore, because a quantum object's wavefunction is spread out across many 'classical' states you could propose a simple initial condition that includes all the complexities as emergent structures in the quantum superposition of these states. All the observed complexities can be regarded as partial descriptions of a simple fundamental reality: the Universe's wavefunction. The quantum Universe has two basic laws: a deterministic one of temporal evolution and a simple one that picks an initial wavefunction for the Universe. Hence, the quantum Universe satisfies strong determinism. The physical laws permit exactly one cosmic history of the Universe, albeit one described by a wavefunction that superposes many classical trajectories. There is no contingency in what the Universe, as a whole, could have been, and no alternative possibility for how it could have started and every event, including the first one, is explained. The entire wavefunction of the Universe for all times is pinned down by the laws."

"Mr Falco, regardless of what you have said concerning the universe and the quantum laws that govern the cosmos, we as human beings are completely free because God has given us free will. Our brains in a sense are like computers, but our minds that operate through the brain are completely free. To conclude... in Him we are free indeed, regardless. Having said that, even if freewill is an illusion, that does not disprove God's existence. Free or not, He has to exist... period."

Alexis rubbed his forehead. He asked meekly, "Okay, fine... Tell me this then. Can you prove that God exists? What evidence do you have for your belief?"

"Well, when one looks at physics, the philosophy of human consciousness, evolutionary biology, mathematics, one automatically, logically, knows that God has to exist... Now, why does the natural world always obey the laws of mathematics? Mathematics is the fundamental world reality that drives the universe. God via his eternal power controls the laws of mathematics which he inscribed in nature, a universe composed of three independently existing worlds - mathematics, the material world and human consciousness. Now how can physical atoms and molecules, for example, create something that exists in a separate domain that has no physical existence: human consciousness? It is indeed a mystery that lies beyond science. Thus, only theology can explain it... The workings of human consciousness are miraculous, and God given.

Like the laws of mathematics, consciousness has no physical presence in the world; the images and thoughts in our consciousness have no measurable dimensions. Yet, our nonphysical thoughts somehow mysteriously guide the actions of our physical human bodies. This is no more scientifically explicable than the mysterious ability of nonphysical mathematical constructions to determine the workings of a separate physical world. The supernatural character of the workings of human consciousness proves that God must exist, an all-powerful supernatural being. Now, to make it easier for you, I will break it down. The proofs for God's existence are as follows:

The Creation demands a Creator. The universe has not existed forever. Rather, the universe, and time itself, had a beginning in the Big Bang, about 15 billion years ago. Science confirms that there has been no past eternity of matter! But how then, did the universe arise? Did it come from nothing? If so, how…? Science can demonstrate that the universe began, but by itself it cannot reveal what or who caused that beginning. God set life into motion via the Big Bang, a tiny speck of superheated space that contained enough energy to create all the stars and galaxies. The equations of general relativity lead to 'singularities' of infinite curvature, most notoriously in black holes and at the Big Bang at the beginning of the Universe. Furthermore, not only do we find predictable physical laws throughout the universe, but we also find tremendous evidence of intelligent design. The human body for example, shows insurmountable evidence of design. Thus, if we find design in the universe, we naturally expect a designer. To conclude, it takes much greater faith to be an atheist than to be a theist. God is the greatest scientist of all.

Life demands a life-giver. Scientists have tried in vain to create life from non-life but have all failed! The law of biogenesis states that life can only come from life. Even under highly favorable conditions of a laboratory, these soups have failed to produce anything remotely resembling life. One problem is that they produce only a random distribution of left and right handed pre-biotic molecules… Life chemistry demands that all the molecules be either right or left handed. With all our learning and technology, we cannot even come close to bringing life together in the lab.

Laws demand a lawgiver. Science has discovered that our physical universe appeared from nothing. When the universe came into existence, all the laws of physics and chemistry were intact; they did not evolve. Everything had to be 'just right' from the very start. Everything from the values of fundamental forces like electromagnetism and gravity, to the relative masses of the various subatomic particles, to things like the number of neutrino types at time 1 second, which the universe has to 'know' already at 10-43 second. The slightest tinkering with a single one of the scores of basic values and relationships in nature would have resulted in a universe very different from the one we inhabit. Thus, all life in the universe was orchestrated, fine-tuned. Now, science has found no reason for the many laws of physics and chemistry, and for the many precise values and relationships, to have come into existence exactly as they are. Remember, these laws were in existence at the first moment of creation. The existence of such marvelous and predictable laws in nature points to a master intelligence and Lawgiver."

Alexis rubbed his forehead again, deep in thought. The Theologian continued...

"Now the law of decay, the second law of thermodynamics says that all life in this universe will cease, this includes the death of the entire universe itself. This is due to increasing disorder and dissipation of heat. This fundamental law affects virtually everything that happens in our universe. Furthermore it's important to note that order came into the world, the law of decay right from the onset, right from the very beginning of time."

Seconds of silence fell as the Theologian paused for breath.

"Mr Falco, immortality is not possible in this universe since the universe itself will eventually die without God's intervention. The second law of thermodynamics guarantees that physical beings cannot live eternally. However God is the elixir of life. Thus, to know him is to be eternal but from a spiritual perspective. Now for my next point! Please indulge me. Although God had created previous hominid species on earth, modern humans were the first to possess a spirit. This is key...! It gave modern man, the capacity to communicate with God. Man could now have a relationship with the Creator. However it is important to note that God had to give man a choice. True love always requires this. God's ultimate plan was to have relationship with mankind without the influence of evil..."

Alexis looked at the man, both admiration and conflict emanating from his eyes.

"Tell me," he suddenly asked, his mind drifting, "How would you as a believer in God counteract the eternity of matter theory that is, the universe has always existed. All the citizens of Mars hold this view rigidly?"

"As mentioned, the second law of thermodynamics holds that over time, under normal circumstances, all systems left on their own tend to become disordered, and corrupted. In other words all things are subject to decay, deterioration, living or not, biological, or mechanical, and finally, are destroyed. This process cannot be avoided; death itself is a manifestation of this law. It is the immutable metaphysical law of the universe."

The Theologian paused momentarily.

"Mr Falco, the entire universe is unavoidably proceeding towards cosmic death. This life-death cycle clearly reveals that there had to be a beginning to everything in the universe including the universe itself. Considering this, the eternity of matter theory makes no sense. God is the genesis of life, the creator. He dwells in eternity, outside the sphere of time and space."

"So what's your view on evolution?" Alexis asked.

"Atheistic evolution makes no sense, but theistic evolution does. Evolution the highly complex process says that disordered, dispersed, and lifeless atoms and molecules spontaneously came together over time, in a particular order resulting in the formation of very complex molecules, proteins, DNA, etc. God was the mechanism behind this process. He has to be. Atheistic evolution basically says life, as a whole, simply evolved by itself under natural conditions. But the second law of thermodynamics contradicts this. No highly complex organic molecule can ever form spontaneously but will rather, disintegrate. To summarize, naturalistic/atheistic Evolutionism... evolution that removes God from the equation requires that physical laws and atoms organize themselves into increasingly complex and beneficial ordered arrangements over time. The second law of thermodynamics says this is not possible. Highly complex, ordered arrangements tend to become disorderly over time and less complex. In other words, there's a downhill spiral at work regarding life throughout the universe."

Alexis was tired but his mind was alive with thought. The expression on his face and the glow in his eyes said it all.

"Mr Falco it's time for me to go but I'll leave you with this... We all live on the edge of eternity. Life can cease at any moment. You were designed with a purpose that purpose is to know God. In fact everything in the universe is designed with a purpose. Teleonomy, information stored within the genes of a living thing is one of the greatest proofs of God's existence. Remember Matter, itself, is not creative."

A few weeks passed... Alexis was now home. He stood on the balcony of his apartment on the fiftieth floor. He gazed into the night sky, cigarette in mouth. Hard rain fell. Lightning and thunder lit the sky. The profound discussion he'd had with the Theologian had left him questioning life, the universe, and its meaning. It was time to make a definitive choice. This choice would require a serious life change. Even the people born on Mars would need to hear this message, even though terra no longer recognized them as human. *'Human meant to have a spirit, a soul regardless of where you are born,'* he thought. He pondered for a while and decided it was time. Inching to the balcony he dropped his cigarette and watched it fall towards the city below...